IF SCAR MCCALL CAN'T KEEP HER COOL, THINGS WILL TURN WILD, AND DANGEROUS VERY QUICKLY

THIS IS NO ORDINARY SCHOOLGIRL, AND NO ORDINARY CAT BURGLAR

TAMSIN COOKE'S ACTION-PACKED FOLLOW-UP TO 'THE SCARLET FILES: CAT BURGLAR'

HIGH STAKES, HIGH DRAMA— A THRILLING PAGE-TURNER

WILL SCAR EVER LEARN TO CONTROL HER SHAPESHIFTING POWERS?

TARGET:
THE DAGGER OF EZTLI

CLIENT:
DESCENDANT OF THE DAGGER'S CREATOR

ORIGIN:
MEXICO

CENTURY:
SIXTEENTH

MATERIALS:
OBSIDIAN, TURQUOISE, JADE,
SHELL, AND ONYX

MARKINGS:
THE HANDLE SHOWS A WARRIOR KNEELING
IN PRAYER, WITH A SMALL BIRD IN
HIS OPEN MOUTH

CONDITION:
GOOD, SLIGHTLY CHIPPED BLADE

VALUE:
PRICELESS

GLOSSARY OF AZTEC TERMS

ACHCAUHTLI

Aztec name meaning leader

CHICAHUA

Aztec name meaning strong

EZTLI

Blood

NAHUALLI

Spirit animal born at the same time as you.
Sometimes you see it in dreams, in shadows,
or—if you are very lucky—you see it in the real
world. Said to have the same characteristics as you.

NAHUATL

The language of the Aztec people

To Dad and my sister Pia,
for always being there for me.

OXFORD
UNIVERSITY PRESS

Great Clarendon Street, Oxford, OX2 6DP

Oxford University Press is a department of the University of Oxford.
It furthers the University's objective of excellence in research, scholarship,
and education by publishing worldwide. Oxford is a registered trade mark of
Oxford University Press in the UK and in certain other countries

Copyright © Tamsin Cooke

The moral rights of the author have been asserted

Database right Oxford University Press (maker)

First published 2016

British Library Cataloguing in Publication Data
Data available

ISBN: 978-0-19-274261-2

1 3 5 7 9 10 8 6 4 2

Printed in Great Britain

Cover and inside illustration: abeadev/Shutterstock.com

THE SCARLET FILES

MISSION GONE WILD

TAMSIN COOKE

OXFORD
UNIVERSITY PRESS

CHAPTER ONE

My heart thrashes. Thin beams of red light zigzag across the room, blocking every path. My target, the dagger, lies on the other side.

I take a deep breath. *Come on! I can do this!*

Fists clenched, I step over the first beam, my body dipped low to miss the one above. Dropping to the floor, I roll sideways under the next two sensors. Climbing to my feet, I leap over another. My trainers crash to the ground but I don't have time to worry. Lifting my foot, my shoelace dangles millimetres from the light. Swooping it higher, somehow I miss the sensor. Deeper into the grid, I squat low, stretch high and soon the dagger's within my sight. Two beams to go. With every muscle tight and tense, I duck under the laser. It flickers.

WOOOHAAA. The alarm screeches.

Noooooooooo!

The main light turns on.

'I really thought you were going to do it this time,' says Dad, switching off the alarm.

Silence fills the room. I was so close.

'I don't suppose you'll let me try again?' I say, finally.

Dad shakes his head. 'It's past midnight. We're driving to Scotland in a few hours. I need some sleep. You need some sleep.'

'Does this mean I can't . . .' The words fall away.

'You know you can't come in the house with me,' says Dad, softly. He leans against the doorway. 'I need you as lookout. If I trip the alarm tomorrow, someone has to warn me the police are coming. But that was a good go. You got far.'

Not far enough!

'How many other thirteen-year-old girls could achieve that?' he says.

I shrug. Dad set up the tripwire system in our lounge last week. We've been practising ever since. Not that he needs to. He achieved it first go.

'Isn't there any way you can cut the power on the grid so there's no alarm?' I say. That's our normal trick.

'I would if I could, but the alarm is linked to the nearest police station. If the link is broken, the police have to check it out.'

'The Dagger of Eztli is valuable then, isn't it?'

'Priceless. We can't afford mistakes.'

I look away. When he says mistakes—he means me.

'Scar, you know I was lookout for your mum when I first joined her out on the job.'

My breath hitches. I can't believe it's been over three years since she died. And I can't believe Dad's talking about her. He hardly ever does.

'Lookout is an important job,' he says. 'You have to be reliable, trustworthy. You can't move from your spot.'

'Fine, I'll do it!' I say, a little harsher than I intended.

An extra crease appears in his forehead. 'Our client is paying us a lot of money for that dagger.'

I take a deep breath and ask, 'It's definitely his then?'

Dad stares at me in surprise. 'Are you doubting my checks?'

I try to keep my face blank. He hasn't always been so thorough in the past.

'I've found evidence that one of his ancestors made it. He has a clear legitimate claim,' continues Dad.

'Then why doesn't he go to the police? Why us?'

'You're being very curious all of a sudden,' says Dad, his eyes narrowing. 'But if you must know, he doesn't trust them.'

'Why?'

'That's none of our business.' He heaves a large sigh and rubs his forehead. 'I think we're both very tired. Let's go to bed.'

'You go. I need a drink first. I'll be up in a minute.'

Dad nods. 'Well, don't be too long and don't have a hot chocolate. It's too late for that.' He walks past me and pats my shoulder. Our version of the bedtime hug.

3

Helping myself to a glass of milk, I lean against the kitchen counter. I hear Dad getting ready for bed upstairs, when my eyes dart towards the lounge. What if I had one more go? But then I think about tripping the alarm. Dad would kill me. Or worse—he'd ban me from the heist altogether.

My jaws clench. Dad has no idea what I'm capable of. Maybe if Mum was here, I'd be able to talk to her.

I need to see Ethan. He's the only one who knows my secrets.

Slipping through the backdoor, I breathe in the cold air and tiptoe round the side of the house. I run as quietly as possible along our cul-de-sac until I reach the tall oak tree in number four's garden. My fingers grasp the familiar branches. In no time at all, I'm three quarters to the top, creeping along the bough leading to an open window. I jump into Ethan's room. Considering how often he stays with his gran, I thought he'd try to redecorate. But it's still covered in flowers. Even in the darkness, I make them out.

'Ethan,' I whisper. 'Ethan,' I whisper again, louder and sharper.

'Arrghh!' squeals Ethan, like a strangled guinea pig. Leaping out of bed, he snatches something long and thin off the floor and waves it wildly in my direction.

'It's me—Scar,' I hiss, jumping out of reach.

He lowers his arms. I can see what it is now. A cricket bat.

'Are you trying to give me a heart attack?' he says.

'I thought you were expecting me,' I lie. 'Your window's open.'

'My window's always open. Gran keeps the heating on.'

'Why do you have a cricket bat by your bed anyway?' I ask.

He throws it onto his crumpled duvet. 'In case someone like you turns up.'

I don't say anything but I know the real reason. It's in case someone we previously stole from turns up.

Ethan switches on his bedside lamp and checks his watch. His face fills with horror. 'What are you doing here?'

'I couldn't sleep.'

'So . . . you thought you'd stop me from sleeping too?'

I hesitate. 'I failed the grid again.'

'Oh Scar, I'm sorry.' Suddenly Ethan's standing in front of me, his arms outstretched as if he's about to . . . wrap them around me?

I leap backwards. 'What are you doing?'

'Giving you a hug.'

'Why . . . why would you do that?'

'To make you feel better.'

'Don't you know me at all?'

Ethan grins and drops his arms. 'You're right. Physical contact was possibly the worst thing I could have tried. It's just I thought you were sad.'

'I'm not sad. I'm angry! Last summer I hot-wired a

car, rescued Dad from kidnappers, and he doesn't even remember.' I shake my head. Not that it's his fault since I wiped his memory with ancient Aztec dust. 'Why did I give him that Aztec powder? If I hadn't, I might be the one in the house and Dad would be lookout.'

'If you hadn't, your dad would know about the Aztec bracelet and your transformations.'

Ethan's words silence me. He means the ancient bracelet a client paid my dad to steal. I put it on my wrist and my life hasn't been the same since. It got sucked straight into my bloodstream and since then I've been able to transform into wild animals. A jaguar and an eagle so far.

I sit on the edge of Ethan's desk, putting my feet on his chair. 'It's a bit mad though, isn't it? We're after another Aztec artefact—this time a dagger.'

'Your dad must have a great reputation in Mexico.' Ethan yawns and glances at his bed.

'The hero of Mexico—returning treasures to their rightful owners.' I pause. 'Do you think the Dagger of Eztli has superpowers too?'

'I looked it up. It was a sacrificial dagger for humans and animals.'

'Not animals!'

He snorts. 'Humans are all right to sacrifice then?'

'Not really,' I say. 'But animals?'

'I read it was ceremonial. Not actually used.' Ethan yawns again. 'Have you had another dream about the bracelet?'

I shake my head. There's only been one dream. I was

6

Achcauhtli, the highest of all Aztec priests. Standing in a temple with four others, we melted gold and spilled our blood, giving our Nahuallis—our spirit animals—to the bracelet. Aztecs believed every person had an animal twin born at the same time as them, giving them guidance.

Ethan rubs his eyes. 'Maybe if you left my house and went back to sleep, you'd have another dream.'

'Why do I want another drea—? Oh. I get the hint.'

Ethan smiles sheepishly. 'I'm just really tired.'

'Yeah, OK.'

I climb onto the windowsill and reach for the nearest branch when Ethan says, 'Scar.'

Still crouching, I twist around.

'I hacked into your dad's laptop again and rechecked his facts.' Ethan is an amazing hacker. He can get into any computer without being seen. He's the whole reason I can keep tabs on Dad. 'That dagger belongs to Delgado. One of his ancestors made it. He's been searching for it for years,' he says.

'So?'

'So—it's a worthwhile heist. *So* being a lookout is worthwhile too.'

'But I won't be needed.'

'You might. And if you do as your dad says, who knows what he'll let you do next?'

With Ethan's words spinning round my head, I scale down the tree. By the time I hit the ground I'm decided.

I *am* going to be the best lookout there has ever been. I'll show Dad what I can do.

CHAPTER TWO

My legs feel numb. Who am I kidding? My brain feels numb. I've been lying here for only thirty minutes but it feels like forever. Dad must be navigating the grid by now. Once he's through the lasers, he'll be fine. According to his recon, the actual dagger isn't alarmed.

Through my night vision goggles—NVGs—I scan the grounds again. I can't see anyone in the country house, the tree-lined driveway, or the gardens. Apart from the odd hoot of an owl, I can't hear anyone either. But I'm not surprised. The owners aren't due back for another two weeks and, with Dad's careful planning, no one's going to turn up. I squirm on the branch. How exactly does lying in a tree prove my great abilities to Dad?

Longingly, I gaze at the house, when the hairs on the back of my neck shoot up. There's a low rumbling of wheels. My eyes flicker left. Three cars swoop onto the driveway, their headlights off.

Dad! I have to warn him.

I've never used it in real life before, only in training, but now I press the top left button on my watch. Dad's watch will vibrate, alerting him he's no longer safe. Then he'll press a button and mine will judder too. I'll know he's received my signal.

Keeping my eyes trained on the cars, I wait for the shudder. But I feel nothing. I hit the button again. Still no response. The cars stop and nine men dive out. Through my NVGs, I make out their uniforms. Police. Dad must have triggered the alarm. I press my watch again. *Come on, shake!* Then my blood freezes. What if the watches aren't working?

I've got to find Dad . . . but I promised to stay here. Argh!

Four men bolt round the side of the house, while five creep up the front steps. I scan the sidewall, desperate to see Dad scaling down. No sign of him. I should stay in the tree, but what if the police get to Dad? What kind of a lookout am I if I can't even warn him?

Part of me knows I'm doing the wrong thing. Dad would want me to stay safe. But the other part—a larger part—squeals at the thought of proving myself.

I scramble down the trunk and dart to the nearest hedge, glimpsing the police disappearing through the front door. I don't have much time. Hoisting my rucksack onto my shoulder, I creep out.

'Stop. Police. Put your hands where I can see them.'

Somehow I bite back a scream.

'I said, put your hands where I can see them.' The voice is deep, loud, terrifying. There's the soft sizzle of electricity. He has a taser.

Slowly, I lift my arms. My brain goes wild. Did I miss someone getting out of the cars? Are there more of them or is he alone?

His footsteps grow closer. I think I'm going to be sick, when all of a sudden my body warms. My wrist feels like it's being strangled by invisible string. I know what's happening. The powers of the bracelet are kicking in. I'm about to transform, but I can't do it here. Not in front of a man. Especially a policeman. I dive into the hedge, my limbs and muscles liquefying. I'm like a waterfall spewing through the hedgerow. Then just as quickly, I solidify.

Closer to the ground, I sniff the air and pad forwards. Earth, leaves, and the smell of man's sweat drift up my nose. I don't know what I'm doing here, but I know danger is close. Peering through the leaves, I see a human shape. I bare my teeth and a growl rips from the back of my throat.

The human shape stumbles.

Leaning back on my haunches, I leap. With brambles tearing my sides, I hurtle through the air. He doesn't even have time to scream as I push him to the ground. My mouth clamps around his head. The man trembles beneath me, his two hands pushing up against my stomach. He's trying to fight back—the fool.

10

All I have to do is bite—break through his skull—when I hear the crackle of a radio coming from his belt. I stop, saliva dripping down my teeth. What am I doing? I'm not a killer. I lift my mouth and stare into the man's panic-stricken eyes. What's he doing here anyway?

Then I remember. Dad.

I step backwards off his body, not breaking eye contact. If he moves a millimetre, I'll have to hurt him. But the man stares back, frozen in shock. The radio crackles again. This time, I grab it with my teeth, ripping it from his belt and biting down hard. The metal buckles and there's quiet.

I snarl and the man scoots backwards. Then I twist round and hurtle for the house. No doubt he'll get up soon, warn the others. I bound up the steps, thankful the front door is open. Slinking inside, I strain to listen. Voices and shuffling feet come from the floor above and the back of the house. I sniff the air. Dad's smells are coming from the back of the house too.

Creeping across the entrance hall, I pass large portraits and human-sized vases. A door to a corridor is wide open. It's like they're inviting me in. The hallway is narrow with doors veering off to the left and right. Most are shut but Dad didn't bother with those. His smells pull me further down, when I hear voices and footsteps. They're coming this way.

A small wooden table is tight against the wall. Racing over, I squeeze beneath it, my body curling round its twisting legs. I lie low, my eyes shut, hiding any light. I hardly dare breathe as two sets of footsteps approach. By their stench, I know Dad's not one of them.

'Have you seen anyone?' asks a voice. Tinny and crackly. It must be coming through a radio.

'No, it was a false alarm,' replies a man with a thick Scottish accent. His heavy black boots are centimetres away from me. 'I'm calling off the search,' he adds.

Yes!

They hurry past me into the main entrance hall and I sneak out from under the table. Obviously they haven't found Dad, but I still need to check he's OK. Creeping further along the corridor, I follow Dad's lingering smells through a large marble archway. Then I stop and stare into the room. Red beams of light zigzag from wall to wall. But it's what they're guarding that draws me in. An Aztec dagger lies proudly on a stone stand, or a plinth, as Dad would call it.

He didn't take the dagger. He didn't bring a fake replacement so that has got to be the real one.

I inch closer to the nearest beam and smell Dad's scent. But instead of going through the grid, the smell stops. *Where did he go?* Looking around, I spot a metal grate at the base of a wall. An air vent. I rush over. Dad's smells are all over it. He must have escaped when the police turned up. Which is great except . . . Delgado— our client—deserves that dagger.

Gazing back at the plinth, every nerve ending tingles. If I take the dagger, Dad will be amazed. He'll promote me. I won't just be lookout.

Growling quietly, I leap over the first beam of light. I slink under the next two, then jump over the fourth. Keeping my tail perfectly in line with my body, I manoeuvre through the grid. Two beams away from the end, I stop. This is where it went wrong. Heart pounding, I sneak under the laser.

I didn't touch it! I scream silently.

Then I leap over the final red line and head for the dagger. Carefully, I pick it up in my mouth.

WOOOHAAA.

The alarm screeches out.

My heart stops beating. Somehow I manage not to drop the blade. But Dad was wrong. The dagger's alarmed too!

Adrenalin fires my brain to act. Spinning round, I race through the grid, tripping every beam. But it doesn't matter now. Heavy boots are hammering towards the room. Hammering towards me.

CHAPTER THREE

Heading straight for the air vent Dad used, I open my mouth, releasing the dagger. I grab the metal grate with my teeth and yank hard. It falls away in my mouth and I trip backwards. Dad mustn't have screwed it back in.

Picking up the dagger again, I climb into the air vent. Legs bent, body low, I slink forwards. My paws scrape the metal floor. I'm making too much noise but I can't help it. Clawing further into the dark tunnel, I hear shouts and curses from behind. The police have entered the room.

A light flickers through the vent. Someone's shining a torch. Luckily I turn a bend so the beam doesn't hit me. Then the tube buckles and deep bangs reverberate down the metal. I scrabble more frantically, slipping, sliding. The police are following. But surely the vent is an even tighter squeeze for them.

Suddenly I meet a fork in the tunnel, two rectangular tubes going off in different directions. Sniffing the entrances, I discover Dad turned left. I hope he knew what he was doing. Hurtling along, a wave of fresh air hits me. I scrabble faster. The exit must be close. I turn a bend and my insides scream with relief. There's no grate, but the green leaves of a hedge. Dad didn't bother putting the grid back on.

Bursting forwards, I leap onto dry earth. I take a deep breath of cold air, letting it circulate my lungs, when I hear running feet. Is it the police, trying to block the exit? I sprint across the grass.

'What was that?' shouts a voice.

I don't even turn my head.

'Was it a cat?' shouts another.

I expect to hear their feet turn direction to follow me, but they continue running towards the air vent. Still I don't slow down. Instead I head straight for my lookout post—the tree I wasn't supposed to leave until Dad came to fetch me. As I approach, I smell his scent. Oh no. He's been here already.

Will he be at the car? *Please say he's at the car.* Pounding the ground, I race to the perimeter wall. I hear police shouting. They're searching the house, the grounds.

I lean back on my haunches and leap as high as I can. My claws grip onto the top of the wall and I scramble over the side. Our car is parked half a mile away. Running silently in the shadows, a horrid thought hits me. What if Dad's back in the grounds looking for me?

Running even faster, finally I detect his sweat. Stronger than before. And there he is—leaning against the car. I can hear his heart thumping as he stares all around and I know he's searching for me. I stop. He won't recognise me like this. I have to transform back.

Keeping low to the ground, I prowl towards the other side of the car to Dad. Thankfully he doesn't think to look down. I make it to the passenger door and lean on my back legs, my front paws hitting the window. I turn my head to stare into the side mirror, needing my reflection to transform back into a girl. Dark brown noble eyes of a jaguar gaze at me.

Hurry up!

I glare deeper into the irises. At last my body warms, my ears recede. My NVGs, balaclava, and rucksack reappear. But my jaw aches. It's stretched far too wide holding the dagger. I drop my head and the weapon falls, my gloved hands ready to catch it.

'Dad, I'm here,' I whisper.

He leaps into the air, twisting round at the same time.

'Oh, thank God.' He rushes around the car and sweeps me into his arms. It feels so good, so reassuring. So alien. I don't want him to let go.

'I don't know whether to kill you or kill you. You left your lookout post,' he says.

OK—I do want him to let go. He might be smothering me to death. As if on cue, his arms open and I step backwards.

'I'm sorry,' I whisper. 'It's just—'

16

'No time now. Get in the car.'

I nod. We jump into the front seats, my gloved fingers wrapped round the dagger. It feels thick and bumpy in my hands. Without switching on the headlights, Dad drives slowly down the dirt track, trying to make as little noise as possible. We're silent, listening out for other cars or policemen.

Finally, we hit a main road and Dad says, 'NVGs.'

I pull them off, along with the balaclava. It's dripping with sweat. So is my back. I squirm uncomfortably in my seat as the headlights flicker on.

'Now that I know you're safe and I can breathe again,' says Dad, 'I'm wondering whether you understand what a lookout is. You weren't supposed to leave that tree under any circumstances.'

'I know, it's just—'

'So when I managed to get out of the house, I ran straight to you. And you weren't there. I thought, OK, she's seen the police. She'll be at the car. But you weren't. I was just about to go back in the grounds to get you, when you showed up.' His voice raises an octave. 'Where the hell were you?'

Gripping the dagger tighter, I say, 'At first I was trying to find you, to tell you the police were here.'

'Why didn't you use your watch?'

'I did. But you didn't respond.'

'I didn't feel anything.'

'I don't think it's working. Then I went in the house and—'

17

'You did what?' Dad's foot slips off the pedal and the car slows down. 'You went in the house even though you knew the police were there? What if you'd been arrested?'

'I knew I wouldn't be.'

'How?'

Because they don't arrest jaguars!

'What if they hurt you? Have you got any sense at all? At least there's one good thing.'

Actually there's another good thing!

He rubs his forehead. 'Thank God we don't have the dagger.'

'What?'

'I didn't get it. After all those times we practised, I tripped the grid on the second beam. I saw the light flicker and I knew we'd have to come back another night. The police will think the alarm system's faulty and no one was actually there. You're sure they didn't see you?'

My heart thrashes in my ears. 'So . . . you don't want the dagger?'

'No. To have it now would be a prison sentence. The owner of the country house isn't due back for another two weeks so we had *that* window to get the dagger to our client. No one would know it was missing until then.'

My mouth is drier than the Sahara Desert.

'Dad,' I croak. 'There's something I have to tell you.'

18

CHAPTER FOUR

'You have what?' explodes Dad.

This was supposed to be my moment of glory. Instead there's a dullness in my chest, as I tell Dad how I navigated the grid, escaped through the air vent. Obviously missing out the fact that I was a jaguar.

After I finish, silence echoes around the car.

At last Dad says, 'I cannot believe you put yourself in that much danger.'

'I thought I was helping.'

'I know you did.' His voice is tight, as if he's trying to keep it under control. 'But Scar, you are not old enough to make decisions about heists. You can't see the consequences.'

'I thought you wanted it.' My answer sounds so pitiful.

'I did. I do. But I wanted to get the dagger unnoticed; otherwise I wouldn't have cared about tripping the alarm.

I would have raced in and out.' Dad sighs heavily. 'I need you to drive. I'm calling Delgado right now. I need to arrange a drop-off point before news of the robbery hits the media. Before he gets spooked.'

Dad pulls over to the side of the road and we swap places.

'I also need silence,' he says. 'Do you think you can follow that simple instruction?'

'Yes,' I whisper, reaching for the lever under my seat, yanking my chair closer to the pedals.

I drive along the motorway, while listening to the endless ringing on Dad's cheap mobile he bought for this heist. Delgado isn't answering.

'He could be sleeping,' I say quietly.

'Could be,' says Dad, but he doesn't sound convinced. He sighs again. 'Delgado made it perfectly clear that, if the police got involved, the deal was off. I assured him no one would even be aware of the theft for at least two weeks. And by then, he'd be back in Florida.'

'Oh,' I mouth.

With the phone still stuck to Dad's ear, we leave Scotland and enter the north of England. The catseyes in the middle of the road begin to blur and my eyelids grow heavy. I give myself a shake, trying to wake myself up. I should tell Dad. But if I can't even drive a car, how useless am I?

Suddenly my eyes flash open. Dad's hand is on the steering wheel.

'Was I asleep?' I gasp.

'It's my fault. Pull over,' he says, his voice shaky. 'I

should never have asked a thirteen-year-old to drive at four in the morning.'

We arrive home just before lunch. I clamber out of the car and, in a sleep-like trance, stumble to bed. Dad heads to the lounge, still on a mission to get hold of Delgado.

I hear talking. Rolling over in bed, my head and body feel thick and weary. The talking seems to get louder and my eyes open blearily. I look at the digital clock. 18:38. Whoa! I've slept for over six hours.

Dragging myself out from under the warm duvet, I creep down the stairs. Has Dad got visitors? But we never have visitors, apart from Ethan and he's at boarding school half an hour away. Then I realize it's the TV. I step into the lounge to see Dad perched on the edge of a sofa, his eyes glued to the news. A politician is on the screen apologizing for something.

Without looking in my direction, he says, 'It's the headlines.'

Another item comes up. A rare white jaguar stolen from a zoo in Miami. *A jaguar—like me.* My temperature instantly rises. I hate to think why such a creature would be taken.

'Wait for it,' says Dad, just before the image changes to the outside of a Scottish country house.

I recognize it straight away even though I only saw it at night-time. Now there are journalists, not just police, crawling all over it.

Dad rubs his chin. 'I think it's fair to say the story has hit the media.'

'They can't link it to us though, can they?'

'I hope not.'

The screen changes to a hospital and a reporter.

Dad turns to me. 'Did you see a wildcat last night?'

What? I try to make my face as blank as possible. 'No. Was there one?'

'According to the police, one of their men was attacked at about the same time we were there.'

'But he wasn't hurt!' I say.

'I wouldn't know,' says Dad. Then his eyes narrow. 'How would you?'

'I . . . I wouldn't. It's just we would have heard the screams. Did you manage to get hold of the client yet?' I ask, desperate to change the subject.

Dad's face turns even grimmer. 'No. And I don't think I will. Which means we are stuck with a hot item. I'm trying to work out what to do with it.'

'Can't we just look after it for a while? Delgado's going to turn up eventually.'

'I really don't want it in the house, but it looks like there's no other option.'

He walks over to the coffee table and pulls open a drawer. The Dagger of Eztli lies inside. I've seen pictures of it on the internet and held it in the dark. But there's nothing more exciting than seeing a priceless treasure in real life in the light. I hurry over.

The dagger is beautiful . . . if a little creepy. Half the

dagger is the blade, the other half the handle, and the whole thing is about twenty centimetres long. The blade is oval shaped, shiny black, made from obsidian rock. It's slightly chipped, but that's not surprising, considering it's five hundred years old. The handle is the mesmerizing part. It's a warrior on his knees, his body leaning forward towards the blade, as if he's praying. His head tilts upward and his mouth is open with a bird sticking out. I can't tell whether the bird is peeking out or whether the man's just eaten it. The handle is covered in small mosaic tiles made from turquoise, jade, shell, and onyx.

Dad picks up the dagger and puts it into his belt before making his way over to the fireplace. I follow him and we both grab hold of the log burner. Together, we heave it to one side. Bending low, I step into the fireplace where the log burner was and stand up straight, sticking my head and body into the flue. There's not much room for me but it's an absolute squeeze for Dad.

He presses the dagger into my hand and suddenly images fly into my head. Flickering scenes of animals writhing on an altar. An obsidian blade plunging through white fur, white scales, white feathers. Red blood spilling. Without gloves, this dagger feels dangerous. Cursed. It wants to kill. It wants to stab these hearts. I release my grip and it crashes to the floor.

'Tell me you didn't just drop that,' says Dad.

His words are muffled, but they break my dreamlike state. I bend down, take a deep breath, and pick up the weapon. Straight away I see more images of death in my mind. They make me nauseous and all I want to do is drop it, but Dad passes me a torch. I can't let him down again.

I stand up, this time perching on my tiptoes. Shining light onto our electronic safe, I try to see through the violent pictures in my mind. Luckily I don't have to rely on memory. My fingers automatically key in the code and the door swings open. With its delicate tiles and age, I should take more care, but I just want rid of it. I shove the dagger inside and the images disappear. Within a minute, I'm back on the carpet, the log burner in its proper place.

'I'm going to try calling Delgado again,' says Dad.

I'm going to try not to throw up! I'm going to try to forget!

CHAPTER FIVE

The following morning, I head to school, leaving Dad on the phone, still trying to get hold of Delgado. Classes and lunch pass in a blur. I can't concentrate on quadratic equations, *Doctor Faustus*, or my sandwiches. Even now, as I stand outside the science room with the rest of my class, my mind is on the dagger . . . and those images. As much as I try, I can't forget them.

Someone shoves me from behind. Zac! He stretches out his arms as if he's some sort of rock star. And I guess he is. He's the star of our year. Mr Popularity. Captain of the football team. Dark hair, brown eyes, caramel skin. He's in my form and most of my classes, but we've never spoken. I don't think he knows I'm alive. Just how I like it. It's best no one notices me at school. Friends or enemies mean questions.

'This is going to be the best lesson ever!' he shouts.

'What are we doing again?' asks one of his friends.

I don't get to hear the reply for a loud annoying voice drowns it out.

'No way is that true!' screeches a girl from halfway down the corridor.

Glancing right, I see Olivia, another member of the popular gang, gliding through the jostling crowd. Everyone parts to the sides as if she were Moses. I'm about to look away when I realize she's heading straight for me.

Flicking her poker-straight black hair off her shoulder, she says, 'Is it true you're going out with Ethan Riley?'

'What?'

'Is . . . it . . . true . . . you . . . are . . . going . . . out . . . with . . . Ethan . . . Riley?' she repeats slowly and carefully, as if talking to a toddler.

A few girls snigger.

Seriously? She wants to talk about Ethan? He doesn't even go my school but seems even more popular than Zac. All the girls think he's so good-looking. Obviously they don't see him when he wakes up with drool and bed-hair. They don't see how long he spends getting ready *every* morning, afternoon, evening.

Olivia starts again: 'Are . . . you . . . going . . .'

'I'm not going out with Ethan!' I snap. 'Where did you get that idea from?'

'Amanda Taylor told me.'

26

Oh! Amanda from the year above. She and I met in the summer. She's a friend of Ethan's. Definitely not a friend of mine!

'Ethan and I are just friends,' I say.

'I knew it,' says Olivia, breaking into a huge smile. She lifts her head and shouts at the top of her voice, 'They're just friends. Told you he would never go out with someone like her.'

Well, I would never go out with someone like him. In fact, I couldn't care less about relationships. I care about daggers and police and . . .

The door to the biology lab opens and my stomach lurches. The stench of rotting flesh flies up my nose. Saliva pools in the back of my throat. My skin grows clammy.

'I hope you're ready,' says Mrs Jenkins, standing in the doorway.

I buckle over, trying not to breathe through my nose. 'What are we doing today?'

'Dissection,' she replies.

My legs crumple. I'm going to fall. Blindly, I reach for the nearest arm.

'What the—?' Zac stares at me in horror.

'Wahey, look at that. Zac's got himself a girlfriend!' shouts one of his friends.

'Zac and Scarlet forever,' yells another.

The class burst out laughing. Zac wrenches his arm free. From having never paid me the slightest bit of attention, he glares with such venom. But I still need something to hold onto. I grab his arm again. His glare turns to a sneer.

'Don't you like dissection?' he asks.

'Move it, lovebirds,' shouts a voice from behind.

Before I know it, I've been shoved into the room and Zac disappears. The smell of rotting carcasses intensifies. I stumble over to my chair. A dead frog lies sprawled on a chopping board. I feel the sick rising. Vaguely I'm aware of girls squealing, boys laughing.

'Settle down,' shouts Mrs Jenkins from the front of the class.

Suddenly Zac's standing in front of my lab table, smiling smugly, eyes glinting. He snatches the frog off my chopping board and waves it back and forth by its foot. He stretches out his arm until the frog is centimetres from my face. Grabbing hold of a scalpel, he rips through the frog's body. Blood, guts, and the stench of death pour out.

My vision clouds. My sickness vanishes. How dare these frogs be sacrificed for us? How dare Zac make a joke of it? I want to pick him up by the foot. Use a scalpel to tear through his torso.

Then the blade in his hand gleams in the light. Could he use that on me? My wrist tightens. My body heats. I want to bite through his skull. I have to.

'Zac Beaches, what do you think you're doing?' bellows Mrs Jenkins.

But her words seem distant to me. *You're mine!* I lift my arm, ready to grab Zac by the neck. Then I spot the skin on my hand. Bubbling. And I'm jolted back to the present. There's no way I can transform. Not here. Not in front of everyone.

My stool screeches across the floor as I leap backwards, hurtling out of the room. I race down the corridor, my limbs dissolving. I burst into the girls' toilets—thank God they're empty—and head straight for the mirror.

You have got to be kidding!

I look like some sort of mutant. One pointy ear, a black nose, a twitching tail, and my skin bubbling like crazy. My eyes flicker from grey to brown. If anyone sees me like this . . . I shudder at the thought.

Slamming my clawed hands onto the sink, I lean closer to the mirror and glower at my reflection. Hurry up before someone comes in!

At last my pointed ear bubbles back into its normal shape, the tail disappears, and the claws recede. My nose becomes pink, my eyes turn grey, and my skin smooths. I fall against the sink and take a deep breath just as an older girl walks in.

'Are you all right?' she says. 'You look like you're going to be sick.'

'I've been better,' I croak.

I manage to get out of the room. That was too close. Automatically I head back to the lab. Then stop outside the door. There's no way I can go back in there. In fact, the way I'm feeling, there's only one place I want to be. I just hope Dad's managed to get through to the client and is in a better mood. I'll tell him I feel sick . . . which is the truth anyway.

I cycle home as fast as I can, but as soon as I reach our driveway, I stop. There are two cars parked on it. One belongs to Dad but I don't recognize the other. Is it Delgado's? But Dad wouldn't invite him to the house, surely. I climb off my bike and push it onto the lawn, before easing the front door open. I hear female giggling.

Moving silently into the hallway, I peer into the kitchen. My lungs constrict. Dad is sitting at the breakfast table, but he's not alone. A woman, with short brown hair, painted nails, painted face, is staring into his eyes, holding his hand. Oh God! It's worse than the dead frog. Dad has her lipstick on his lips!

As if sensing me, Dad looks up. His eyes widen and he jerks his hand away.

'Scar!' he yelps.

I don't wait to hear or see anything else. Spinning around, I charge upstairs to my room. I lock the door but Dad could unpick that. Grabbing hold of my bedside table, I drag it across the floor. The alarm clock and light crash to the ground, unable to free themselves from their wires. Ignoring them, I push the cabinet flat against the door.

There's a loud knock but I'm not answering. The handle turns and the door rattles but it can't move.

'Scar, let me in,' calls Dad. 'We need to talk.'

Again I don't reply. Tears stab the corner of my eyes. I feel sick, exhausted. School was hell. Now this?

'Juliet's gone,' he says.

So that's her name!

30

'Is that our client?' I splutter.

'No. She's . . . she's a friend.'

Oh really? Kiss all your friends?

'I thought we weren't supposed to have friends,' I hiss.

'Scar, if you would just open the door,' says Dad.

No chance!

I don't want to face him today. I'm not sure I want to face him tomorrow. Needing a distraction, I drop to my knees and pull out the red scrapbook from under my bed. The Scarlet Files, as Ethan calls it. It's full of newspaper cuttings of our family heists. They made the headlines because the police had no idea who committed the crimes. Except they're not crimes. We're helping people. Dad has no idea I have this, for if the police raided our house, this would more than incriminate us. But there's no way I can get rid of it. It's about Mum. Dad. And me. There's no Juliet. No grotesque make-up.

I wipe the tears from my eyes, when a terrifying thought slinks into my brain. Who is Juliet? She could be a policewoman? A former target—someone we stole from?

I have to find out.

CHAPTER SIX

A woman looms over me, her mouth smothered in red lipstick. Cackling like a demented witch, she raises her arm into the air. I stare in horror at the obsidian blade aiming straight for my heart. Wriggling backwards, I crash to the ground.

My eyes flash open. I've fallen out of bed.

With sweat dripping down my back, I lie in a crumpled heap. Taking a few deep breaths to calm myself, I try to get the nightmare out of my head. It's pretty obvious what's on my mind.

I don't want to think about Juliet, but I do want to think about the dagger. Even in my dream, it felt cursed. I check my digital clock, still lying on the floor.

02:30.

Surely Dad's asleep. I climb to my feet, slide the

bedside table away from the door, and slip into the hallway. Gentle snores drift from Dad's room. Creeping downstairs to the dining room, I wake the computer from sleep mode before typing 'The Dagger of Eztli'. Sites fill the screen and I click on them. Ethan was right. The dagger was only used for display. It never killed anything. I should be pleased, but something doesn't feel right. Why did I see those images when I touched it?

Biting my lip, I add the word 'cursed' to Google. My insides quiver as I see one site: *Legend of the Cursed Dagger.*

I hit the page and my blood turns to ice. I read and reread the words. This can't be true. Because if it is, the Dagger of Eztli is pure evil. An uneasy feeling begins to claw at my gut. Does Ethan know the legend? But surely he would have told me . . . or is he hiding things from me? Then the claws extend like a wildcat's. More importantly, does Delgado know? Because what sort of person wants a dagger like this?

Stabbing the keys, I type his full name: Anton Miguel Delgado. Sites about his company—Green Gas—fill the screen. Selecting them, I learn nothing new. Ethan told me this already. Forty-eight-year-old Delgado has petrol stations all over America and is a multimillionaire. He's married to the fashion designer, Melinda Delgado. Apparently I should have heard of her. She creates gowns for the Oscars and other red carpet events. They're a golden couple, known by celebrities.

But as I stare at the pictures of him—greying black

hair, long nose, dark brown eyes—all I see is arrogance. And there's nothing that links him to the dagger. I need to be more specific. I add the Dagger of Eztli to his name in the search engine. Still nothing. I stretch out my fingers. Should I be looking at this from another angle? Deleting the words 'Daggers of Eztli' I add 'animals' and site after site flashes up.

Clicking on the first, I'm drawn to the picture of Delgado. He's much younger than forty-eight in this photo and he's gazing into the eyes of a glamorous woman. The pair of them are holding rifles and crouching behind a dead lion. Blood coats the animal's fur. I look at the caption and clench my fists so tight, nails bury into flesh. They're on their honeymoon. *Who would choose a hunting honeymoon?*

In the article I learn they met on a hunt. Delgado even mentions his Aztec heritage—proudly stating that sacrificing is in his blood. My lungs constrict. Even if Ethan didn't know the dagger's history, he must have known this. He did all the research. My nails dig deeper. Why did I leave it up to him? I can use a stupid computer. I can type!

I choose different sites. Murders of bears, wildcats, rhinos light up the screen. Delgado's smug face grinning over each of his kills. This can't be legal.

Jumping to my feet, I race up the stairs, this time not worrying about being quiet. There is no way a man like Delgado can have the Dagger of Eztli. Together they would be lethal.

'Dad!' I shout, flinging open his bedroom door and switching on the main light.

'Scar! What's happened?' he yelps, bolting upright.

'You can't give Delgado that dagger!'

'I can't . . . what?' He stills, his eyes squinting. 'You woke me up because of the dagger? Couldn't this have waited until—oh, I don't know—daylight?'

'He doesn't deserve it.'

Dad scrapes his hands through his hair. 'Why would you think he doesn't deserve it?'

The words tumble out about the honeymoon, the killings, even the legend, and I'm so pleased when Dad's face turns grim. He's just as angry as me.

'Did you say—his eyes scrunch shut for a second '—you were looking up the client and the dagger on our home computer?'

'Yes—but we can clear the history.'

'A computer expert could unclear that. This is sensitive information. What were you thinking?'

'I was thinking about the animals,' I say, shaking my head in disbelief. *That* is what Dad's worried about? Then I realize he's shaking his head too, looking at me like I'm some sort of wild alien.

'Scar, Delgado paid good money for us to take that dagger. And when I say good money, I *mean* good money.'

'I thought it wasn't about the money,' I snap. 'I thought it was about returning treasures to their rightful owners.'

'It is, and Delgado is the rightful owner,' says Dad, his voice rising. 'Or are you doubting my checks again?'

Then his eyes widen, his face softens. 'This is about Juliet, isn't it?'

'Huh?'

'Do we need to talk about her?'

'No!'

Dad doesn't seem to hear me. 'I met her at work.' For his day job, Dad tests out new security systems and writes about them. 'Her full name is Juliet Flannagan,' he adds.

My nightmare instantly comes back. I remember Juliet looming over me, the dagger in her hand.

'Have you checked her out?' I ask.

'What?' Dad splutters.

'Have you done background checks on her?'

'Oh . . . right!' he says. 'Of course I have. She's got nothing of interest on her record.'

'Neither would you, if someone examined yours.'

Dad looks taken aback for a second. 'Wow! You're even more suspicious than me. And who exactly do you think she is?'

I take a deep breath. 'She could be working for Delgado.'

'She's not!' he says, and by the expression on his face, I know not to mention Delgado again.

'What about the police? Is she working for them?'

He tilts his head. 'Like Ethan's dad?'

My heart stops. 'You know that?'

'Of course I know that. I've done checks on his whole family. And don't get me started on his sister.' He folds his arms. 'Do you not think there might be the smallest possibility that Juliet is a normal woman who likes me for being me?'

I look at the floor. 'I guess there might be that smallest possibility,' I mumble.

Dad rubs his forehead. 'Listen, Scar, I'm really sorry you found out about her this way. I wanted to introduce you to her properly. I know you miss your mum, but Juliet is important to me. And so . . . I invited her over for dinner tomorrow night.'

Blood starts pounding in my ears. I can't have heard correctly.

'Actually she's technically coming tonight,' he adds, glancing at his watch.

Is he completely mad?

'I thought you should meet her sooner rather than later.'

Sooner is not less than twenty-four hours!

'I want you to meet her properly. Get to know her,' he continues.

'I don't want to get to know her,' I say, finally finding my voice.

'We'll be eating at eight.'

'And I don't have a choice?'

'No, I'm afraid you don't.'

CHAPTER SEVEN

Still seething the next morning, I don't want to see Dad. I grab my diary, shove it into my rucksack and hurry out the door. I jump on my bike, but instead of heading straight to school, I go to our local shop first. There's something I have to buy.

A shopkeeper leans his elbows on the counter and doesn't take his eyes off me as I wander up and down the aisles. *I'm not a shoplifter!* I want to yell. I would never do something like that. At last I spot what I'm looking for and pay for it quickly.

It's still early for school and so halfway there I veer off into the local park. Ignoring the pathway, I aim for the trees. I check no one is about, before pulling out my diary and lifting its cover. Inside the hollowed-out pages lies a mobile phone—the one Ethan gave me. He knows never to contact me on it when Dad's home for I'd be so dead if Dad ever discovered I had one. Phones can be traced.

The pouch of Aztec powder is hiding in there too, but I leave that inside. Taking out my mobile, I tap in Ethan's number. I shouldn't be having this conversation over a phone, but what choice do I have? I'll just have to be careful with what I say.

After four rings, Ethan picks up. 'Scar, is everything OK? You never ring.'

'No, everything is not OK.' I fight to keep my voice under control. 'Did you know he shoots wildcats?'

'He?'

'Yes! He!' I say pointedly.

'Oh God!'

'I'm guessing you did then. Did you also know he shoots alligators, crocodiles? In fact anything endangered.'

I hear an exhalation of breath. 'Yeah, I knew.'

My hand squeezes the phone. 'Did you not think to tell me those things? We could have—' I think frantically what to say to not incriminate us '—we could have kept the whole thing from Dad by intercepting emails.'

Ethan clears his throat. 'But why would we do that? He's the rightful owner. His ancestor made it. I thought the whole point of your . . . thing . . . was to return treasures back to their rightful owners.'

'But you know what sort of person he is. And his wife.' I take a deep breath, then say, 'Did you know about the legend?'

'Legend?' He sounds genuinely curious.

39

'I found it on the internet.'

'*You* found it?'

'Yeah—I found something on the internet you didn't. And you're right his ancestor did make it.'

'Chicahua—I know that bit,' interrupts Ethan.

'Did you also know that Chicahua was an Aztec warrior who hated his Nahualli? Thought it embarrassing, unworthy. So he had the dagger made and it was blessed by one of the gods. During a full moon'—the taste in my mouth sours—'he killed a rare white jaguar to bond himself to it. He plunged the dagger though its heart and the jaguar became his Nahualli. Since then, that dagger's been used so many times by descendants of Chicahua—each time killing a rare white creature.'

'OK—I never heard that story.'

'It's not just a story,' I say. Forgetting I'm on the phone, I tell him about my visions in the fireplace, explaining with explicit detail the feel of the blade plunging through each different heart.

'All right, all right, I get the picture,' he says, cutting me off.

'That dagger felt cursed, and I mean *really* cursed. I think Delgado wants it so he can choose his own Nahualli.'

Silence.

'Did you hear me?'

'I admit he's not the nicest of men, but Delgado sounds like a trophy hunter—collecting animals. The dagger's probably another trophy he wants. Did you also

40

read the articles saying it was ceremonial? It won't have real powers.'

'Like the bracelet and memory powder have no real powers? Can you explain my visions?'

Ethan sighs. 'I doubt Delgado believes in Nahuallis.'

'I think you're wrong.'

'He hasn't got hold of your dad yet.'

'But he will. So we need to stop him. I have to get the dagger out and I can't move that stupid log burner on my own. When are you next at your gran's?'

With a groan, Ethan says, 'I can come Friday.'

'Can't you come sooner?'

'If I walk out of school, they'll notice.'

'But you'll help me on Friday?' I say. 'Promise?'

'Yes, I'll help you on Friday. But what are you going to tell your dad when he finds out the dagger is missing?'

My heart stops. *Dad will be so disappointed. No—he'll be furious.* 'It's about saving lives. I don't care what he thinks,' I say, hoping Ethan doesn't notice the words catching in the back of my throat.

CHAPTER EIGHT

With the Dagger of Eztli and Delgado churning round my head, I cycle the rest of the way to school. But, turning into the gates, they're instantly forgotten. Normally no one notices I'm alive, but today kids are looking at me. With an uneasy feeling, I chain my bike to the railings. I hear giggling. Glancing over my shoulder, I see a group of girls staring. They turn away quickly but not before they mouth the name 'Scarlet'.

Oh great!

It seems that running out of school gets you noticed. We moved away from my old home, my old school, so I could be invisible. From now on, I can't afford to attract any more attention.

I drop my head, letting my hair fall over my face and head straight for my form room. Avoiding all eye contact, I walk over to my usual seat . . . except some-one's already in it.

Zac!

Two of his friends sit in the chairs either side. *You are kidding me!*

I take a deep breath. *I can deal with this.* I force a shrug, pretending I couldn't care less. This way they may leave me alone, let me blend in again.

But Zac leans back in my chair. He grins smugly and his eyes glint. It's the exact expression he used when waving the frog in my face. Suddenly I notice the scalpel in his hands. My wrist tightens. I feel hot. Deep inside my brain I hear a voice screaming at me to jump on him, rip that smile off his face, grab the scalpel. I'm barely conscious of my lips pulling back in a sneer. But when fear flashes across Zac's face, I'm jerked back to reality. I wrench my eyes away from him and reach into my bag, fumbling. *Come on. Where is it?* My skin will bubble any second. I don't have time to run now. Then my fingers clasp the compact mirror I bought from the local shop. I stare into it.

'Seriously? You're posing?' shouts Olivia, bursting into laughter.

Vaguely I'm aware of others laughing too.

Faze them out, I tell myself, staring even harder into the mirror.

'What have you got be vain about?' says Olivia.

Concentrate on my reflection!

Finally my body cools. I lower the mirror to see

everyone having hysterics. Zac and Olivia more than anyone else. Heat burns again but this is a different type of heat. My cheeks are flaming red.

Clutching his stomach, Zac stands up. 'Are you happy you look all right for me now?'

Think peaceful thoughts . . . happy thoughts . . .

With a clenched jaw, I turn away and walk to an empty chair at the front of the class.

'Oh my God!' says Olivia. 'Did she honestly look at herself in the mirror? Does she think she has a chance with Zac? That is the funniest thing I've ever seen.'

Olivia, shut up, I think, my fingers tightening around the mirror again. *Otherwise I won't look at my reflection and we'll see how much you're laughing then.*

In every lesson, Zac or one of his friends sits in my usual place. I'm seriously thinking about knocking every single one of them out, then force-feeding them the memory powder.

Somehow, I make it to the last lesson. English. Thankfully, neither Olivia, Zac, nor any of their friends are in this class, and I can sit in my usual seat. I try to concentrate on *Doctor Faustus* when I feel a poke between the shoulder blades. I look up sharply. Am I supposed to be reading? But a boy is droning on, his monotone voice killing Marlowe's play.

I look back down when I feel another poke, harder this time.

'What?' I snap, looking over my shoulder.

A girl, who has never spoken to me before, points dramatically to the classroom door. Following her finger, I almost jump out of my seat. Ethan is peering through the small glass square in the wood. What's he doing here? Then a coldness hits my core.

'Miss, can I go to the toilet, please?' I call, my hand shooting up.

Rolling her eyes, she says with a sigh, 'Yes, you can.'

I leap up and shove my books into my bag.

'Not planning on coming back then?' says the girl in the seat behind. Her eyes sparkle and I bet she can't wait to spread the gossip.

'Who knows?' I whisper, darting out of the room. As soon as the door shuts, I say, 'Delgado's contacted Dad, hasn't he?'

Ethan nods. 'Yeah. But it's even worse than we thought.'

CHAPTER NINE

Ethan tugs me down the corridor.

'How can it be worse?' I ask.

'I'll tell you in the taxi.'

'Taxi?'

Then I hear footsteps. Someone's coming down the corridor. I shove Ethan through the door to our right, immediately following behind. Pressing my ear to the door, I hear someone in high heels—a teacher no doubt—walking straight past.

'I've never been in the girls' toilets before,' says Ethan.

'I'm glad to hear it.'

'It smells nicer than the boys'.'

'Ugh! You didn't need to tell me that,' I say, opening the door a little.

The corridor's empty again. This time neither of us

says anything, as we tiptoe out of school. Thankfully, the car park is empty too. I only hope there aren't any teachers looking out of the windows.

We climb into the back of the taxi and Ethan leans forward. 'Can you take us to Primrose Garage, please? It's near Bristol.'

'Yeah, sure.' The driver peers over his shoulder. 'Shouldn't you both be in school?'

'No,' says Ethan confidently. 'We're doing a school report on petrol stations.'

The driver grins, his eyes darting between the pair of us. 'Yeah! Course you are!' With a twinkle in his eye, he puts on the radio. A love song blares out and he grins even more.

I glare at the back of the driver's head before leaning towards Ethan. 'So what's worse?'

Watching the driver, Ethan puts his hand over his mouth and whispers, 'Your dad got an email from Delgado this morning.'

'Nooo!' I mouth.

'Asking your dad to meet him at a petrol station near Bristol. Delgado apologizes for not responding sooner—says he was out of the country on a rhino hunt in Africa.'

Bile rises to my throat.

'But that isn't even the worst of it,' says Ethan. 'Delgado was furious that the police were alerted to the missing dagger, but he really, really wants it, Scar. He asked if he could collect it this week because he needs it

47

for Saturday night to go on top of some stone plinth in his Everglades house.'

"I'm guessing Dad replied?' *Even though I asked him not to.* I feel nauseous.

'He replied straight away. He must have been looking out for Delgado's emails. I think your dad was a bit surprised, though. He didn't think Delgado would contact him because of the police.'

'I wish he hadn't.'

'Your dad suggested they meet today because it's the best time for him. And Delgado was *more* than happy.'

I sink back into my seat when I feel Ethan's eyes burning into my neck. 'Is there more?' I whisper.

Ethan brushes his hand through his hair. 'When I read the email I thought why Saturday night? Is there something significant about that date?'

'Is there? Is it an Aztec holiday?'

'It's a full moon.'

My mouth dries and it feels like the car is spinning. 'Are you sure?'

'I checked on the internet. And I found that legend you were telling me about.'

'So now you believe me?' I mutter, but the words seem hollow. I look out of the window, watching the houses and shops crawl by. 'What time are they meeting?'

'Four.'

I glance at my watch. It's quarter past three.

'Excuse me,' I say to the driver. 'How long is it to the petrol station?'

'About an hour. It's just off the motorway.'

I look through the window again. A cement mixer would overtake us at this speed. 'Can't you go any faster?'

'And break the speed limit?' Peering at me through the rear view mirror, he says, 'Don't you worry about the money. It's a set price. Your boyfriend sorted it out before you got in the car.'

'He's not my boyfriend.'

'No, of course he's not. And you two are really doing a report on petrol stations.'

He laughs at his own joke while I stare at Ethan in horror.

'Better he thinks we're boyfriend and girlfriend than international thieves,' he whispers.

I'm not so sure!

We hit the motorway and finally speed up . . . to seventy miles an hour. I glare at the speedometer on the dashboard. We are seriously running out of time. 'You know seventy is just a guideline,' I say.

'You make me laugh,' says the driver.

I look at the back of his head. How easy would it be for me to knock him out and take over the driving? When suddenly the car lurches forward, throwing us against our seat belts.

'Sorry about that. Everyone still alive?' says the driver.

'Just about,' says Ethan.

'What's going on?' I ask, my heart pounding.

The driver points forward. 'Traffic jam.'

Cars line all three lanes and my heart pounds even

more. 'What's happened?' *Not an accident. Please not an accident. That's how Mum died.*

'Roadworks,' says the driver, pointing to a sign. And I close my eyes in relief, until he adds, 'Looks like we're going to be here for a bit. Might as well sit back and enjoy the ride.'

'But we can't be late.'

'Not much I can do about it.'

The car inches forward and I slump in my seat. I could kill Dad. Still doing a deal with Delgado.

Then everything disappears—Ethan, the driver, the countryside.

I'm surrounded by four wooden walls. No windows. I stare around the room in terror. I have to get out of here. Storming past the stone altar in the centre, I slam my body against a wall. The room shudders but nothing breaks. Panic rising, I know I'm trapped. I scrape at the wall, with my claws extended. I make deep grooves but there's still no sign of daylight. Letting my paw fall back to the ground, I lower my head. Then my throat dries. I'm staring at a white paw covered in dark spots. A white jaguar.

Just as quickly, the paw vanishes.

I'm back in the car with Ethan beside me. He's elbowing me like crazy, but I can't think about him. What the hell just happened?

'Scar, you're transforming!' he hisses. 'Get out!'

My eyes dart to my bubbling hand. Frantically, I fumble with my seat belt, vaguely aware of Ethan rummaging in his bag.

Shoving a phone in my hand, he whispers, 'Ring me as soon as you can. The garage is called Primrose and it's on the A38 off Junction 22.'

I open the passenger door, leap out of the car, and thrust the phone into my back pocket.

'Where are you going?' yelps the driver.

I can't even answer. Ethan will have to think of an excuse. My wrist is getting tighter. My muscles are turning fluid. I have to make it to the hedge otherwise the drivers and the passengers will see. I look for a hole but the thicket's too full. I have no choice. I charge straight through the brambles. They scratch my skin, my clothes, but I hardly feel them. I'm liquefying. Just as I get to the other side, my wings stretch out and I soar into the air. I've transformed into an eagle. The sky beckons as power surges through me. I feel so free. I can fly anywhere. Everything is clearer and with my peripheral vision I can almost the see the world behind. My eyes dart downwards to the rows of stationary cars. Thank God I'm up here away from all that, unlike poor Ethan.

Ethan!

I can't just fly where I want. I have somewhere to go. Flying into the wind, I sweep through the sky, following the motorway. The tops of the cars look like never-ending caterpillars and the cones stretch on for miles. Ethan's going to be stuck there for a while. Keeping an eye out for signs, my mind spins. I was a white jaguar in a wooden room. Was I really there? Or was it some crazy hallucination? Or am I just going mad?

With these thoughts going round my head, I almost miss my turning. At the last second I spot Junction 22 and veer off. Following the new road, I soon come to a garage. Primrose. A silver car pulls out of the forecourt and my eyes zone in on the minute scratch on the bonnet. Dad's car. My heart leaps to my mouth. I'm too late. Dad must have handed the dagger over already.

Except . . . maybe Delgado's still here . . .

My eyes flicker over the remaining cars in the forecourt. I've no idea which one is his, and, for all I know, he's employed someone else to pick up the dagger. Praying he turned up himself, I swoop lower, peering into one windscreen, then another.

An old man. A mother with her toddler.

Delgado!

Even though he's wearing aviator sunglasses, there's no doubt it's him. His dark hair, littered with grey, swept to one side. His long nose. The same self-satisfied smile he used when crouching over a lion. Thank God he turned up himself. The dagger must be important to him.

I follow Delgado out of the petrol station, along the A38. Glancing at a sign, my stomach twists. We're heading to Bristol Airport. I might be able to fly but I can't compete with a plane. Then, to my relief, he turns left into an industrial estate. I read the sign: Stavener Industrial Park. From high above, I watch him navigate the maze of roads, passing old buildings, depots, car parks. He reaches the far end of the estate and pulls onto an empty gravelled drive. It's beside a large corrugated iron ware-house covered in graffiti. Old and abandoned.

On the opposite side of the road is a derelict build-ing, with smashed windows and boarded-up doors. A sign, Plumbing Goods, dangles from the roof. I land on a streetlight between the two as Delgado climbs out of his car. He looks shorter in real life than in the pictures on the internet. But even from here I can see his thickset neck . . . and the pulse throbbing in his soft flesh. I could rip it out, sever an artery. For this is the man who has killed so many animals. I could stop him from hurting more.

My muscles tense. That would make me as bad as him. I just need the dagger.

My eyes zoom in on the bag he's clutching. Brown paper—the sort Dad likes to use. I dive towards him, claws outstretched, ready to tear the bag away. Then he looks up. For a second only, I catch my reflection in his glasses. The yellow eyes. The deadly beak.

My body begins to melt.

CHAPTER TEN

Twisting in mid-air to get away, I catch the expression on Delgado's face. White. Jaw open. Terrified. Sprinting to the warehouse, he leans in towards an electronic lock in the door. The warehouse isn't that abandoned, then.

His body blocks the numbers. Even though my insides are dissolving, I flap my wings as hard as I can. Their power is weakening but I manage to lift a few centimetres. My eyes zoom in on his frantic fingers. 7943. The code of entry. He pushes the door. With melting wings, I dip lower. He heads straight for an alarm on the opposite wall. My eyesight is becoming more human. Straining to see his fingers, I watch him tap 3284.

The door shuts. I struggle through the air, around the corner of the warehouse, before slamming to the ground.

I land on my left leg. I stretch it out in front and wiggle my toes—so glad nothing's broken.

Slumped against the wall, I wonder what just happened. Delgado looked straight at me and was scared. Does he know what I am? Does he think I'm a Nahualli? In fact, what is his Nahualli?

Suddenly I remember the white paw in the wooden room. My chest feels like its being squeezed by an invisible lasso. Is that the animal Delgado plans to kill? Is he keeping it in a cabin somewhere? I relive the jaguar's panic, its fear.

I *have* to get to that dagger . . . which means I *have* to get in the warehouse.

I run through the numbers in my head. 7943, 3284. 7943, 3284. Then I squirm. Something lumpy's sticking into my bottom. Feeling my back pocket, I could hug Ethan. He gave me his spare mobile.

I dial his number and after two rings he answers.

'Are you OK?' he asks.

'I'm fine,' I lie. 'Where are you?'

'Still on the motorway. It's a nightmare but at least we're moving now,' says Ethan. 'Did you get it?'

'No, I was too late. But I know where it is. And I'm not at the garage. I'm in Stavener Industrial Park. It's further up the A38 on the left. There's a warehouse at the end of it—covered in graffiti. Looks abandoned but it's not. I need you to come here. Don't park on the drive; that will be too obvious. There's a plumbing place opposite—Plumbing Goods. Go there.'

'What should I tell the driver?'

'Anything you like,' I say. 'Listen—there's a code to get in. 7943. Repeat after me—7943.'

'Tell me you're not going in.'

'Repeat the code. 7943.'

'Scar, wait for me.'

I hear the front door of the warehouse open. 'Got to go,' I whisper, shoving the phone back into my pocket.

The front door shuts. I sink into the wall as far as possible. But whoever is out there doesn't come this way. Their feet scurry across the drive. Carefully, I peer round the side of the wall to see Delgado open the door to his car. The brown paper bag isn't with him. Climbing inside, he keeps checking the sky. And with his head craning upwards, he wheelspins out of the car park, disappearing out of sight.

I wait a minute more, before creeping round to the front of the warehouse. I can't see or hear anyone. But as I stare at the digital keypad, I bite my lip. This is possibly one of the most reckless things I have ever done. No planning. No tools. Not even a pair of gloves. Without my rucksack on my shoulder, I feel naked. Plus I'm in my school uniform. If anyone catches me, they'll know where I'm from.

Then the white paw flickers through my mind again. Who knows when I'll get another chance like this?

Before I can change my mind, I tap in 7943. I hear a click and push the door open. The alarm blinks red on the opposite wall. Argh! What was the code? It definitely started with a 3. I close my eyes, trying to visualize

Delgado's fingers. 3274. Opening my eyes, I type in the number, but the light's still red.

Come on—think. I visualize his fingers again.

3284.

I take a deep breath and try once more. The light switches to green. I step inside and the door slams behind me. Loud. I half expect Delgado to come charging back.

But now what? Where would he hide the dagger?

I push open another door and my muscles quiver. *Not that smell . . . please not that smell . . .* I force my legs to move and soon I'm in a room the size of an aeroplane hangar. Clothes hang off portable railings. If you can call them clothes. I buckle over, desperately trying to swallow hot saliva pooling in the back of my throat.

Clutching my stomach, I stagger forwards.

There are coats and capes made from skins. Tiger. Snow leopard. Jaguar. Bear. Cheetah. The room begins to spin. I spy snake handbags, alligator shoes. It's an abattoir. My legs tremble. Tears sting my eyes. The vile stench is overpowering. But I can't be sick. They'll know I've been here. They might even test it for DNA.

I swallow hard. Then a brown paper bag on top of a table at the far end of the room catches my eye. The dagger! I make for it when I hear the front door open. Even in my dazed state, I know I have to hide. Is it Delgado? Has he come back?

Scrabbling across the room, I dive behind a floor-length leopard coat. *How many creatures died for this?* I wonder, as the second door opens.

'Is someone in here?' booms a deep American voice. 'Delgado, did you switch off the alarm?'

So it isn't Delgado, then.

His feet step into the room. I want to shuffle back but I'll make a noise. The rotting carcass of a coat dangles millimetres from my face. My head spins all the more. I try to breathe through my mouth, when cigarette smoke pours down my throat. Oh God. I need to cough. I clasp my lips together but the urge is getting stronger. My stomach starts convulsing and a cough explodes from my mouth.

The man's feet run straight towards me.

'Who's there?' he shouts.

My heart thrashes. My body heat rises, but where's my burning wrist? I need claws, talons, fangs. I grab my wrist with the other hand and squeeze, frantically hoping to kick-start the bracelet. Nothing.

Spinning around, I run straight into a tiger coat. The fur wraps itself around my face. It feels so wrong. So evil. I stumble backwards, tripping over the leopard coat railing. It crashes to the ground. And standing in front of me with a look of absolute shock is a security guard. His cigarette dangles from his fingers, the ash dropping to the floor. In his other hand is a gun—pointing straight at me.

CHAPTER ELEVEN

'Who the hell are you?' he says.

I can't speak. Silenced by the silencer on the end of his gun. Just what kind of guard is he?

He puffs on his cigarette. 'Are you alone?'

I manage to nod.

'Stand up!'

With shaking limbs, I climb to my feet. He towers over me. My brain feels fuzzy, my body disconnected. If only I could get away from the stench of death.

'You're a kid! Think it's some kind of joke to break into a warehouse?' Then he looks around. 'How did you get in?'

I open my mouth, ready to lie, but cough. The tiny trail of smoke seems to be on a mission for my lungs.

He drags on his cigarette again. 'Is this bothering

you?' He flicks the ash, so it lands at my feet. 'What's your name?'

I cough again.

'I said, what's your name?' He thrusts the gun closer and I automatically step backwards.

'Olivia,' I croak, the name slipping out. Uh oh. If he looks at my blazer and remembers my name . . .

'What are you doing here?' he says.

'I hate fur.'

The man snorts. 'So . . . you're an animal activist? What are you planning to do? Destroy them?'

I hadn't thought of that, but what a fantastic idea. I clench my fists. 'You know this is illegal. These animals are endangered.'

'*Were* endangered. These ones are dead.'

'Only because you killed them,' I spit, my fear turning to anger.

He takes another long drag of cigarette. 'I didn't personally. My boss did.'

'All of them?'

'His wife may have helped.'

My nails dig into my palms. 'What are they going to do with them? They can't sell them. They're from protected species. It's illegal.'

'Now that is none of your business.'

'I'm making it my business,' I say, looking him straight in the eye.

The guard bursts out laughing. 'And what exactly are you gonna do about it? Even if I didn't have a gun, I don't think you have the greatest chance against me.' He cranes his thick neck. Muscles crack. 'How old are you? Eleven?'

'Thirteen!'

Keeping his eyes and gun trained on me, he pulls out his mobile phone. I feel the blood drain from my face.

'Are you calling the police?' I ask.

'I don't think my boss wants the cops turning up, do you?' says the guard, flicking ash in my direction. I jerk my arm out the way. 'But I'm not quite sure what to do with you. I don't like killing kids. I'd like to chuck you out but you've seen this place. And you're an animal lover.' He says the last words like it's the worst crime in history.

'What if I promise not to say anything?'

'What? A pinky promise?' he says with a snigger, wiggling his little finger. 'You ain't in school any more, hon.'

'So who are you calling?'

'My boss.'

'Delgado,' I mouth.

Suddenly the gun's touching the side of my head.

'How do you know Delgado?' he demands.

Did I honestly just mouth his name? He pushes the gun further into my temple. My heartbeat races so hard, I think it might explode.

'I don't know him! I've heard of him—that's all!' I yelp, shaking my wrist. Why won't this bracelet work when I need it?

The guard starts tapping a number into his phone. He's not looking at me. I kick him as hard as I can between

61

the legs. His body crumples and he drops the mobile. I jump on the phone and feel it crunch beneath my feet. Then I run straight for the door.

He thunders after me.

Racing past tiger skins, jaguar skins, I keep my eyes on the door handle. My head feels so faint, so thick. If I can just make it out of this room. His feet close in. I smell tobacco breath. I'm not going to get to the door. And so I grab the nearest thing—a metal pole balanced on a clothing rail. I swing it high in the air behind me. It connects with something. There's a sickening crack, followed by a grunt. Spinning round, I watch him fall to the floor, the gun slipping through his fingers. His head hits the ground and blood trickles out. Oh God!

With cold sweat dripping down my back, I drop to my knees beside him. I lean over his head, my cheek to his mouth. His tobacco breath tickles my skin and I lean back in relief. He's alive. Then I almost laugh. He let go of the gun but he's still clasping his cigarette. The last remnants of smoke waft away.

Now what should I do? He knows Olivia's name. Knows a thirteen-year-old girl was here.

Suddenly I think of the brown pouch in my school bag. Will Ethan be at the plumbing place yet? Leaping to my feet, I push through the two doors until I'm out on the drive. I hurtle across the car park, when I see Ethan running across the road. He's here! Then I see the taxi driver following closely behind.

'Are you OK?' asks Ethan.

'I'm fine,' I say. 'I just need my—'

'What happened to you?' says the driver.

What's wrong with me?

'Your top,' says Ethan.

I look down and slam my arms across my chest. Patches of blood cover the top of my shirt, my blazer.

'It's not my blood,' I say.

'Then whose is it?' says the driver, his eyes darting about.

'Did someone have a nosebleed? Were you helping them?' says Ethan. I know he's trying to help the situation, but the look of panic on his face gives him away.

'Yeah, I was—'

But the driver is shaking his head, pulling something out of his pocket. 'I don't know what you two are up to but it isn't good.'

I stare at his hand. You have got to be kidding? Another mobile phone. Dad's right. They are an absolute menace. Trying to keep my voice calm, I say, 'Who are you going to ring?'

'The police.' His eyes flicker to my top. 'And maybe a paramedic. Is someone hurt in the warehouse?'

My muscles tighten. The police can't come here. I'd love them to find the furs but they can't find me.

'Put the phone away,' I say.

'Please,' adds Ethan.

The driver walks away from us. 'You two stay here. One day you'll thank me.' And he taps a digit. Nine, I'm guessing.

My wrist strangles. Heat floods through me. My limbs begin to melt.

'I said, put the phone away!' The last word comes out as a roar.

CHAPTER TWELVE

Standing on all fours, I glare dangerously at the man. His eyes widen and he turns to bolt, but I stretch out my legs and leap. I open my mouth, ready to bite, when I hear: 'Scar, don't!'

Ethan's words slice through me. I spin in mid-air. Instead of claws tearing through the driver's shoulders, my body slams into him. He crashes to the ground.

'Please', he whimpers.

'I'm not going to hurt you,' I say, but a growl breaks out.

The driver's body shakes. His eyes roll backwards and I know he's fainted.

This may be our only chance. I race over to the taxi on the other side of the road, glaring into the side mirror. *Come on. He could wake up any second.* As if sensing the urgency, my body returns in record time. I whisk open a back door and pull out my bag, fumbling for the Aztec powder hidden in my diary.

Ethan's kneeling beside the driver.

'Out of my way!' I shout.

He moves aside, as I open the pouch. There's not much left. Probably just enough for the driver and the guard. But then what? If someone else sees me transform, I won't be able to do anything about it.

'Are you OK?' says Ethan. 'You're staring into space.'

I grimace. I don't have a choice. From now on, I can't let anyone see me transform. Ever. Hoping this is the right thing to do, I pinch some powder between my thumb and forefinger. The driver's mouth is open in shock. Perfect. I drop some yellow dust onto his tongue and it sizzles like bacon in a pan.

I take a deep breath and say, 'You took two children to an industrial estate. You don't know who they are or anything about them. It's a normal day for you. You did not see a jaguar. The girl had a nosebleed, which is why she has blood on her blazer and shirt. You'll sleep for a little while, but when you wake up, you'll wait for the children and take them back to their schools.'

Then I stand up and look at Ethan. 'We have to get him over to the taxi.'

'What? We've got to carry him all the way over there? Across the road?'

I bite my lip. 'All right, I have a better idea. Can you find his keys?'

Ethan scrambles in his pockets and fishes out a set.

'I'll be right back,' I say.

Hurtling over to the plumbing car park, I jump into the taxi. Soon I'm pulling the cab onto the drive next to the warehouse. I climb out and grab the driver under his arms.

'You get his legs,' I say.

'What if he wakes?' says Ethan, taking hold of his ankles.

'You don't want to know.'

'Let's not wake him then,' says Ethan hurriedly, and together we manage to stuff the man in the driver's seat.

'I hate to say this—but we have to do this to someone else now.'

Ethan looks horrified but follows me over to the warehouse. The front door is shut and I lift my hand to type in the code on the electronic keypad. My hand hovers in the air. Oh no! I can't remember the number.

'7943,' says Ethan.

Of course—that's it! I throw him a quick smile before tapping in the code. The lock clicks and I push open the door. Luckily the alarm on the other side of the wall is still flashing green. I've completely forgotten that number and I didn't tell it to Ethan.

I enter the massive room and the stench of death hits me all over again. My head begins to thicken. *Concentrate*, I tell myself, kneeling beside the guard sprawled across the floor. I heave a silent sigh of relief. He's still out cold. When I glance at Ethan, though, he looks even more horrified. He's staring at the gun.

'Did he threaten you with that?' he whispers.

I nod.

Ethan wobbles a little and for a moment I think he's going to faint, but then he crouches beside me. I glare at the guard's closed mouth. Then I lean over, pinch his nose, and cut off his air supply. The man opens his mouth, gasping for breath. Ignoring Ethan's groans of disgust, I drop the rest of the powder onto the guard's tongue. Too late to worry about the empty pouch now.

As the powder fizzes, I say, 'Nothing strange happened today. You checked the warehouse and it was empty. But you felt so sleepy you decided to take a nap. While you were sleeping, you fell off the chair and hit your head. That's why it's bleeding.' I stand up. Then add, 'Oh, and you hate fur. You think it's cruel and want nothing more to do with it.'

I take a chair from a nearby table and position it beside the guard.

'Right—I need you to help me destroy these furs,' I whisper. 'If the animals can't wear them, no one can.'

Ethan shakes his head. 'We can't do that. They'll know someone's been here. They might check for fingerprints. You just tampered with that man's brain so he forgets about you.'

I grind my teeth. He's right of course. 'We'd better clear up then, so no one suspects a thing.'

We rush around the room. My skin crawls every time I pick up a dead animal and put it back on a hanger.

At last the room looks like I found it. Organized death. I hurry over to the brown paper bag lying on the table, when I remember the white paw in the cabin. My insides twist.

'Ethan,' I call, and he comes over. 'Something happened while I was in the taxi, just before I transformed.'

'Was that when you were in a trance?'

'Is that what it looked like?' I know I don't have much time but I have to tell him about my 'vision' or whatever it was.

Ethan's jaw drops lower and lower. 'So you're telling me you saw what the jaguar saw?'

'And felt what it felt.'

'But how? Why?'

'I don't know. I feel like there's some sort of link between us.'

'Because you become one?'

'Maybe,' I say. 'But there's one thing I'm sure of. Delgado wants that white jaguar to be his Nahualli.' Ethan's eyes grow wide and I can see it in his face—he agrees with me. 'But Delgado won't be able to sacrifice it now. We've got the dagger. I saw him bring it in here. He left in such a hurry, he probably forgot to put it in a safe.'

I pick up the bag and my stomach drops. The bag is the right size, right shape, but it feels too soft, too light. Shoving my hand inside, I pull out fur. I let go straight away and it falls to the floor. I'm vaguely aware of something clanging to the ground and rolling away. Metal possibly. But I pay no attention. For sorrowful eyes are

69

looking up at me. It's a scarf made from a fox.

Ethan puts his hand on my shoulder. 'Look at this,' he says breathlessly.

There's a small silver flash drive lying in his palm.

'Where did you get that?'

'It fell out of the bag.' He looks down at me in earnest. 'I've got my laptop in the taxi. We could copy it. See what's on it.'

I glance at the guard, still out cold. 'Do it quickly.'

Ethan hurries out of the warehouse. Less than a minute later, he's back, sliding the flash drive into his computer.

'It's loading,' he says, just as the guard rolls over.

'Be quick,' I say, not taking my eyes off the man.

The guard mumbles something. *Please say he's dreaming.*

Then all of a sudden someone shouts, 'Kids, where are you?'

The taxi driver has woken up. He can't come in here.

'I'll go,' I say. 'Come when you're done.'

I sprint out of the warehouse to see the driver on the tarmac, rubbing his head.

'Have you got everything for your school report?' he asks.

'Yeah. We were just interviewing some people in there. Etha—my friend—is finishing up. He'll be out in a minute.'

'Great,' says the driver. 'I don't normally nap in the day.'

'My dad does,' I say.

'So does mine,' says Ethan, smiling, walking towards us. I hope the taxi driver doesn't spot the sweat pouring down his face. 'I got everything,' he adds, tapping his laptop.

'Did you leave everything like we found it? Close both doors?' I ask.

'Yeah. We're ready to go.'

We climb into the back of the cab and hardly speak during the whole journey. We both gaze at his laptop. Tell me there's something about the dagger in there otherwise this whole thing was a waste of time. I didn't even get to destroy the furs.

As the driver pulls up outside the private school, Ethan hands him a massive bundle of notes.

'What's that for?' says the driver. 'We agreed on a price.'

'It's a tip. We kept you much longer than we thought.'

Ethan must be feeling guilty. I suppose I should be too.

Ethan checks his watch and says, 'Eight o'clock. I'm just on time.'

'Eight!' I exclaim. 'I'm supposed to be home for dinner NOW.'

'Your dad won't care,' says Ethan. 'He's not like my housemaster.'

Cold waves of panic spread through me. 'He'll care this time!'

The driver drops me off at school and I grab my bike.

I pedal so fast down the streets, my legs scream with pain, but I don't slow down. Skidding onto our driveway, I groan in horror. Juliet's car is already here.

I'm late and covered in blood.

CHAPTER THIRTEEN

As quietly as humanly possible, I open our front door and slip inside. Halfway up the stairs, I hear Dad's voice, unmistakably angry.

'Tell me you have a great reason why you're late.'

Turning around, I say, 'I had to—'

'Is that blood?' he asks.

'I had a nosebleed.'

'Oh Scar.' His voice eases. 'Are you all right?'

Part of me is relieved. The other part squirms in guilt. 'Yeah. I walked into a wall.'

'How?' Then he shakes his head. 'Never mind. Tell me later. There's someone I want you to meet.' I climb back down the stairs and follow Dad into the dining room, where Juliet is standing, a glass of wine in her hand. She's wearing even more make-up than last time and a tight dress revealing every lump and bump.

'You must be Scarlet,' she says warmly. But her eyes flicker nervously.

Dad nudges me.

'Hello. Sorry I'm late. I had a nosebleed.'

'Oh, poor you.' Her eyes glimpse my top and her nose wrinkles. 'Don't you want to get changed?'

'I'm fine like this,' I say, dumping my bag beside hers. My lips twitch. She's going to have to stare at the blood for the whole meal. In fact, what is the meal? There's a horrid smell drifting into the room.

Juliet sips her wine, leaving lipstick marks on the glass. 'Ever since eight o'clock your father has been getting crosser and crosser, but I've been telling him—teenage girls have their own time zone.' She smiles sweetly. Too sweetly.

'I'm learning all about teenage girls,' says Dad. 'I'll go bring the plates in now. The lasagne is ready.'

I avoid his eye. Is that the horrid smell? Did Dad burn the food because I'm late? I sit opposite Juliet at the dining table and fold my arms. I think this might be the first time we've ever eaten in this room. Normally we eat in the kitchen. Silence ricochets off the walls. I stare at her and she fidgets uncomfortably.

'So . . . your father tells me you love animals. Do you have a favourite?' she asks.

'Not really.'

'Are you sure? Isn't there one you really like?' she says.

What is this? The Inquisition? But I know she won't give up, so I say, 'All animals are just as important as each other. But if I had to choose, I guess it would be the jaguar.'

Dad reappears with three plates.

'Ooh, it smells delicious,' says Juliet, as he puts one down in front of her.

Liar!

He sits next to her while Juliet peers at my plate.

'Yours looks different,' she says.

'Scarlet's a vegetarian,' explains Dad.

'Like Mum was. But Dad's always eaten meat,' I say. 'He doesn't think there's anything wrong with eating dead animals. So I guess you have that in common.'

A loud silence fills the room again. Dad glares at me. Juliet puts down her fork.

He clears his throat. 'So? What were you two talking about while I was in the kitchen?'

'We were discussing our favourite animals. Scarlet's is the jaguar,' says Juliet.

'And yours is?' asks Dad.

Fluffy bunny? Cute little puppy?

'The snake,' she replies.

I sit in almost silence. I answer questions—Dad's eyes will burn me alive if I don't—but I refuse to say anything more than 'yes' or 'no'. The meal seems to drag on forever and ever, but finally we get to pudding.

Then a phone rings.

My blood freezes.

Ethan's spare mobile from my rucksack. I stare at Dad, who stares at Juliet. The phone rings and rings and rings. I'm going to kill Ethan.

'Aren't you going to get that?' Dad asks Juliet.

'It's not mine,' she says.

I swallow hard. I'm going to be more dead than those animals in the warehouse.

'Well, who else could it belong to?' says Dad. 'It's not mine. And Scarlet doesn't have one. She's not allowed.'

Juliet shakes her head and laughs. 'Oh, silly me. Of course it's mine. I have different ringtones for different friends and I haven't spoken to Michelle for ages. I forgot that was hers. Dan, I don't suppose you can get me a glass of water?'

'Of course,' says Dad, jumping to his feet.

As soon as he leaves, Juliet whispers, 'Turn off your mobile now.'

I don't need telling twice. I rush over to my bag, scrabbling for my phone and press the off button. I get back to my seat just as Dad returns with a jug.

'Would you like some water?' says Juliet, smiling at me.

'Yes, please,' I say, trying to smile back. I can't believe she covered for me.

The rest of the meal goes quite well. I make polite conversation and Dad seems pleased. We wolf down the brownies and, as I watch the pair of them, I realize Dad looks happier than he has in a long time.

At last Juliet stands up and says, 'Well, I have work

tomorrow. I really should be going.'

'I'll see you to the door,' says Dad. 'Scarlet, you can go to your room now if you want. I can see Juliet out.'

Hmm. So you can kiss her goodbye. That is going too far.

'That's all right, Dad,' I say with a treacly smile, getting to my feet. 'I'd like to see her off too.'

'You don't have to,' says Dad.

Suddenly he looks nervous. Why?

Juliet's eyes dart between the two of us and she looks confused too. 'Dan, are you going to get my coat?'

'Are you sure you don't want to go to bed?' he asks me.

'I'll wait,' I say, watching him carefully.

He walks out of the room and returns seconds later with a coat. The smell I detected earlier pours up my nose. Not another fur! Not more death! Not after the warehouse! My stomach cramps and I buckle over.

'Are you all right?' says Juliet in alarm.

In that instant I forget she covered for me. I forget she makes Dad happy. I grab onto the chair to stop falling over.

'What the hell is that?' I scream. My head feels dizzy.

'My new coat,' says Juliet.

'Scarlet, please,' says Dad, his eyes flashing.

'It's chinchilla,' I say.

'Yes, I know,' says Juliet.

'And do you know that they skin sixty chinchillas for one coat? Sixty animals died for you!'

77

Juliet's face pales. 'I . . . I didn't know that.'

'Well, you do now. So go on. Put on those dead animal skins. I hope their rotting carcasses make you feel pretty.'

Dad grabs me by the shoulder. 'Upstairs now!' he roars.

I charge to my room, desperate to get away from the smell. From death.

'I'm so sorry,' I hear Dad say. 'I should have warned you, but she's—'

'A teenager,' says Juliet, her voice shaky.

I don't wait to hear anything else. I slam the door to my room and shove my furniture back in front of it. But Dad doesn't come upstairs. He doesn't check to see if I'm OK.

CHAPTER FOURTEEN

My eyes flash open as I remember last night. Juliet. The phone call. My mobile!

I bolt upright. I need my bag before Dad wakes up. Pulling the bedside table away from my door as quietly as possible, I creep downstairs.

Rats!

The TV is on in the lounge. Dad must be up. Tiptoeing, I pick my bag off the dining room floor.

'You're up then,' says Dad.

I turn to see him standing in the doorway, his face grim. Does he have supersonic hearing or some amazing Nahualli who tells him of my every move?

'I was getting my bag. I need to get ready for school.'

'You don't need to do anything else?'

I frown, not understanding.

'Like apologizing, maybe?' he adds.

Oh . . . that!

'You know I hate fur,' I say, but I shift uncomfortably. She covered for me last night. If I were her, I would have told on me. Oh God—has she? 'Did she—erm—say anything?'

'Not really,' says Dad.

So . . . she still hasn't given me up. 'I am sorry,' I say. Then I look Dad straight in the eyes. 'But you knew I'd get mad. That's why you tried to send me away.'

He smiles thinly. 'Just because she wears fur doesn't make her a bad person. You seemed to be getting on quite well with her.'

'Well . . . she wasn't as bad as I thought she'd be.'

'Cor, that's high praise coming from you. And if it makes you feel any better, she hasn't got the coat anymore. She got rid of it.'

'Good!'

Dad snorts. 'Anyway I was watching the news. Seeing if there's anything more on the Scottish house. Do you want to watch it with me?'

I follow him into the lounge.

'I gave Delgado the dagger yesterday,' he adds. 'It's a relief not having it in this house, I can tell you.'

But I hardly hear Dad's words. I stare at the TV. A white wildcat is on the screen. And underneath is the title: Albino jaguar still missing from the world-famous Zoo Miami.

Every nerve ending throughout my body seems to

tingle. Of course—how did I not work this out earlier? Delgado's kidnapped the missing jaguar, and he's keeping it in a wooden shack somewhere. The terror and panic of being trapped comes back to me and I start shaking uncontrollably. I grab the remote and turn up the volume.

'It's still a mystery where Storm is. The five-year-old jaguar was born and raised in Zoo Miami, and although he's used to his handlers, he's known to be wary of strangers. His twin, Thunder, misses him terribly.'

The image changes to a white jaguar lying on a rock in the middle of an enormous enclosure. Trees, a lake, grassland. Not four wooden walls. My panic changes to anger. The camera zooms in towards Thunder's face. She lifts her head and her eyes are filled with such sorrow.

My fists clench.

I'll get Storm back to you. I promise.

Why did I get the dagger for Delgado in the first place? I should have left it in Scotland.

On cue, as if to taunt me, the TV screen changes to the country house. My anger turns to repulsion. I sense Dad approach and know he's looking over my shoulder.

'New evidence has turned up regarding the missing dagger,' says a reporter.

I stiffen and hear Dad's harsh intake of breath.

'Sergeant Farris remembers seeing a masked burglar just before he was attacked by a wildcat. The police are looking into this new line of enquiry,' continues the reporter.

I didn't think it was possible, but I seem to be shaking even more.

'I thought you said you weren't seen,' says Dad.

'I wasn't.' I keep my face fixed to the screen so he can't see my expression. 'That could have been you.'

'I wasn't seen either!'

We watch in silence but learn nothing new. It seems the police are still baffled. Finally another news item comes up and I turn to Dad.

'We have to get that dagger back from Delgado.'

'Oh Scar,' says Dad, smiling softly. 'The police aren't going to find us. If you say they didn't see you and I know they didn't see me, they're making it up for something to say on the news. I bet they're no closer to finding the dagger than before.'

'I'm not scared of being caught. I just don't want Delgado to have it.'

Dad's smile drops. 'Do not start that again. Anyway, it's too late. He's already gone back to Florida.'

'Then we need to go to Florida. Before Saturday.'

'For the last time—Delgado deserves it.' I open my mouth to speak, but Dad lifts his hand to silence me. 'I'm afraid we couldn't even if we wanted to. I have another heist this weekend.'

What?

Normally a job takes weeks of preparation. Ethan hacks into Dad's laptop so we can vet the client, check the plans. And as a rule, Dad only does one heist a month.

'That's quick,' I say.

'I know. But there's an opportunity to get back a Chinese statuette. It should belong to Mr Rogerson but at the moment it's in a large banking corporation.'

'How are we going to get it out?' I ask.

Dad takes a deep breath. 'I'm afraid *we* are not. I don't think I can trust you enough to take you along.'

Excuse me???? If he punched me in the gut, it would hurt less.

'After you left your lookout post, I'm not sure I can trust you,' he says.

'Are you serious? I got the dagger.'

'I am very serious,' says Dad. 'You showed me that you can't follow instructions. I told you explicitly not to leave your post. And you moved. I can't worry about you when I'm on a job. I have to be able to concentrate on what I'm doing.'

'But I'm your lookout.' That word doesn't sound too bad now I've been demoted to . . . to . . . nothing. 'Who's going to watch your back now? Who's going to be your assistant?'

'I managed to get by before you. And I think you will learn more if you miss this one out.' He rubs his forehead. 'I'm going to speak to Ethan's gran this morning and see if you can stay with her for the weekend. I'll be back Monday evening.'

'You're punishing me, aren't you? Because of last night.'

'It's nothing to do with last night.'

I turn away in disgust. Dad's leaving me with Ethan's gran, while he's off away somewhere.

Then a thought detonates in my brain.

Fifteen minutes later, I'm back in the park, halfway to school. I get off my bike and pull out my phone. I have to get hold of Ethan. With trembling fingers I switch it on, about to make a call, when texts start pinging.

I scroll through them. My throat burns.

Could this day get any worse?

CHAPTER FIFTEEN

You are not going to believe what I found out on the flash drive—those clothes in the warehouse are for Melinda Delgado's underground fashion show.

Happens every 4 years with clients from here, the US, Russia, China . . .

Animals killed to order. Client says they want an Amur leopard dress. Delgado hunts it, then she 'creates'!!!

Headlining outfit: a South China tiger cape. They think it's such a coup they managed to hunt one down. I looked it up—only 30 left in the wild. 29 now!

I can't wait a second longer. I dial Ethan's number.

'You got my messages, then?' he says, as soon as he picks up.

'A South China tiger? Do they not know they're heading for extinction?'

'I think that's the point.'

'But how can they have a fashion show with any of theses animals? They're protected,' I splutter.

'The show is kept hidden,' explains Ethan. 'They have them every four years in different locations. This time it's in an exclusive holiday resort in Miami, on a tiny island. Invitation only. The whole island is the hotel and they've booked it up, so, apart from the staff, there'll be no prying eyes.'

'When is it?'

'This Sunday afternoon. They must be shipping out the clothes now.'

I think back to the railings full of skins. 'We have to stop this. You have to stop this. Go to your dad, give him the flash drive.'

'He'll want to know where I got it from.'

'Then do it anonymously.'

'I can't. Your . . . your dad's on the flash drive too.'

It's like the world is spinning. Somehow I manage to utter, 'Does . . . he know about the fashion show?'

'No,' says Ethan quickly. 'He's on there because of the dagger.'

For a split second I feel relieved. Then anger takes over again. 'I shouldn't have listened to you. I should have destroyed the furs.'

'They would have just hunted more.'

Heat flushes through me. More than ever I feel sick I helped Delgado.

'You won't believe the guest list,' adds Ethan. 'There

are politicians, a chief of police—'

'Sorry—what did you say?'

I hardly hear him for there's a loud yapping coming towards me. I look down to see a pug hurtle though the trees. The tiny dog snarls and attacks my shoe.

Where have you come from? And what have I done to you?

Trying to listen to Ethan while he tells me the monstrous guest list, I look around for the pug's owner. No one's here. I shake my foot gently, hoping to pry the dog loose, when all of a sudden the pug vanishes. As do the trees, the earthy ground, the sky. Ethan's voice silences.

I'm back in the four wooden walls. I know I'm trapped. I've got to get out . . . but I feel so sleepy. I try to lift my head but it seems stuck to a cold stone. I manage to lift a paw for a second but that too falls back down. The walls seem to close in. There's a shadow—a man in front of me. He's holding something long and sharp, and he's chanting like a maniac. Everything seems so blurry. I want to sleep . . . but I have to escape. Angrily I give a short sharp growl. The man puts down the pointed knife and the four walls disappear. I'm back in the park, the phone in my hand.

The pug whimpers. She scoots backwards.

My body is so hot, and my wrist feels like someone is strangling it—tighter and tighter. Before I even gasp for breath, my muscles, skin, limbs melt. Then harden again. I'm much lower to the ground. The pug turns and runs, her tail firmly between her legs.

But she can't get away from me.

In two strides, she's in my mouth, wriggling, enticing me to bite. One clamp of my jaws is all it will take. The perfect breakfast.

Then she squeals.

Oh God! My mouth opens and the pug scrambles away.

I have got to get control over this!

I look around but thankfully no one is in sight. Sniffing the air, I can't smell anyone either. *Please say no one saw me change.* But now—I have to transform back. I have to talk to Ethan.

I look at the ground and see my rucksack on the floor. I mustn't have been holding it when I changed. Gripping the zip between my teeth, I pull back my head, but the whole bag lifts off the ground.

Argh!

With a paw, I try holding the bag down and yank the zip again. The pull tab rips away in my teeth. You're kidding me! I don't have time for this. My claws slice through the fabric and I nose through the books, pencil case, and old letters until I find the mirror. I stare at my reflection. All I can see is one large deep brown eye of a jaguar staring back at me. Then my limbs begin to melt and my eye flickers from brown to a grey-blue. And soon I'm standing on two feet by my ripped bag, the mobile phone in my hand.

'Ethan, are you there?' I ask, but the line is dead.

Quickly I redial his number.

'What happened to you?' he says immediately. 'All I could hear was barking and then there was nothing. Thought you might have been eaten.'

More like the other way round!

'I went into the jaguar's head again,' I say. 'I was in the cabin with a man. I think it was Delgado.'

'You went in another trance?'

'Yeah, but this time it was different. The jaguar is drugged. I could feel it. He's been given something to make him sleep. He's still scared, trapped—but not with it.'

'The vision just happened? You didn't kick-start it at all.'

'No. One minute I was on the phone with you and the next I was in Storm's head.'

'Storm? You know its name.'

'His name,' I correct. I tell Ethan about the news item. For a moment Ethan's silent and I let the words sink in. Then I hear him exhale.

'I think you're right,' he says finally.

'I know I'm right. Which means we *have* to get to Florida before the full moon on Saturday. We *have* to find that dagger and we *have* to rescue Storm.'

CHAPTER SIXTEEN

I wait for him to say something. Anything.

'What do you think?' I ask, at last.

'When do you want to go?'

'Friday.'

'And come back?'

'It doesn't matter exactly when . . . but it would be good if we could get back before Dad returns from his next heist. That's Monday evening, so—'

'Wait! What next heist?'

My gut churns a little. 'Hasn't he mentioned it on his laptop? He's after a Chinese statuette.'

'There's nothing on his laptop and I looked last night.' Ethan hesitates. 'So let me get this straight. You want to go to Florida and back in three days—a nine-hour journey each way—and find a ferocious wild animal and the dagger in between?'

'We don't have to be back by Monday.'

'That's all right, then!' he says with a snort. 'But you still want to go to Florida and find a dagger and a jaguar that could in fact be anywhere.'

'You're the one who read in the email that he wants it for his Everglades house. You're the one who realized he's planning a sacrifice.'

'I know but—'

'Ethan,'—I try to keep my voice under control—'we can't do anything about those animals we found in the warehouse. They're already dead. But we can do something about Storm. We can save his life. And it's our fault Delgado has that dagger. If I'd known what sort of person he was, I would never have done it.'

'So it's my fault for not telling you?' says Ethan quietly. 'Not exactly.'

'You do know that, if we take it from him, we're stealing? We're not returning a treasure back to its owner. We're committing a crime.'

I pause. Then push the guilt to one side. 'It's worth it. It was a crime giving it to him in the first place. He's going to use it to sacrifice an animal.'

I can almost hear the cogs turning in Ethan's brain, when other boys start shouting his name in the background.

'I've got to go,' he says.

'No. Wait—'

'I'll think about Florida, I promise,' he says, hanging up.

I thought he'd say yes straight away. As I glare at the phone and throw it in my bag, another thought hits me. All those treasures Dad and I returned—what were they used for? Are Dad and I on the side of good or are we helping horrid people commit horrid acts?

Holding my ripped bag under one arm, I cycle one-handed all the way to school. I chain my bike to the school railing, desperately trying to ignore the other kids whispering and pointing.

'Scarlet,' says a grown-up voice.

I can't ignore an adult. Turning around, I see the head teacher walk towards me. This can't be good.

'Can we talk in my office, please?' she says.

Meekly I follow her into the building, past staring kids, staring teachers. Great! This time last year, no one even knew my name. We enter her room, which is remarkably small considering the size of the school. I haven't been in here before.

'So,' she says, sitting behind her desk, 'do you know why you're here?'

I look up at Mrs Constance. 'No,' I say.

She smiles kindly. 'I've been hearing a few reports from teachers that you aren't always turning up to class. And when you do, you're leaving halfway through.'

Ah! That!

'I've only done it a couple of times and only this week.'

'A couple of times is too many,' she says, leaning forwards. 'Up until now, though, you haven't put a foot wrong, which makes me wonder whether there is something going on. Is anyone or anything bothering you at school?'

'No.'

'Anything at home?'

'No,' I say again.

She clasps her hands together. 'We are here for you, Scarlet.'

'I know.' I hesitate. 'Have you told my dad?'

She shakes her head. 'No, but I have thought about it. And I've decided that if you miss one more lesson, I will. He needs to be informed.'

'I won't miss anymore. I promise,' I say. 'It was just a lapse.'

'That's good to hear.' Mrs Constance stands up and opens the door for me.

The corridors are empty. Darting into the toilets, I pull out my mobile phone and text Ethan:

Got to be home Sunday night.

Within seconds, a text pings back.

Are you completely mad????

Possibly, I think to myself as I walk to form room.

Stepping into class, I see Zac is in my usual place again. I hoped he'd found someone else to torment. I shrug and pretend not to care, when he pulls out a mirror. My jaws clench. He holds it in front of his face and starts pouting.

Is he *doing* me? Because I don't pout.

Sniggers scorch my ears. I look around the room

and see his friends, each holding a mirror, each posing. Olivia's doing the same, although I think she is actually doing her make-up.

'Is everything OK, Scarlet?' asks my form teacher, as I hover by the door.

Is she blind? Can't she see the mirrors?

For a moment, I consider saying no, everything is *so* not fine. But through gritted teeth, I say, 'Everything's great!'

In each lesson there's at least one person with a mirror. And everyone else seems to be watching my reaction. I'm not sure how they see it, though, as I'm forever facing the floor, hiding behind my hair. I think I now know every dirt mark and crack ever formed in these school grounds.

The last bell rings. With relief, I stuff my books inside my ripped bag, when I see there's a text on my phone.

I read it and have to stop myself from squealing.

Tickets booked for Florida. We go late Friday night. Come home Sunday. You owe me forever!!!!!

CHAPTER SEVENTEEN

Thinking about Florida and trying to come up with a plan helps me endure the next two days of school. I am sick of people staring, talking about me, mocking me with mirrors. Why can't they ignore me like they used to?

The final bell rings and I'm out like a shot. Head down, I hurtle through the streets until, with a great sense of relief, I open my front door. I'm greeted by two packed suitcases sitting on opposite sides of the hallway. Enemies facing each other. Dad's and mine.

Oh hell! Dad must have got mine out of my room. Please say he didn't open it.

'I'm home,' I shout, the quiver in my voice noticeable even to me.

'That was quick,' says Dad, stepping into the hallway. 'I brought your bag down for you.'

I wait for the explosion.

'What have you got inside? Rocks?' he adds, with a grin.

My muscles unclench. 'School books. I'm doing this big project. I've been to the library and got loads of books out. There were so many and I didn't know which to choose. *Scar, shut up! You're rambling!*

'You know you have a key? You could always pop home,' says Dad, grinning even more.

'Oh—I never thought of that.'

Leaning against the doorway, Dad's face turns sheepish. 'Listen, Scar, I'd hoped to take you over to Mrs Riley's, carry your bag for you. But she rang an hour ago, very apologetic. She's had to pop out for a while and won't be back until seven. She says she's going to spoil you after that.' He rubs his forehead. 'But I could do with leaving now. My plane goes in a few hours and you know how long it takes to get through airport security.'

'Where are you going?' I ask.

'Spain.'

'Oh.'

An awkward silence fills the room.

'So, you'll be OK going to Mrs Riley's on your own?'

'I'll be fine,' I say. 'Will you be OK doing a job on your own?'

Dad's lips twitch. 'I'll miss you, but yes, I'll be fine.' Taking the handle of his suitcase, he says, 'I hope you have a great time over there. And be good. It's very kind of her to look after you.'

'I'll be good and . . . I hope your job is successful.' But as these words come out of my mouth, I realize I don't mean them. I want Dad's heist to fail. I want him to see how much he needs me. *Wow! I really am a horrid person!*

'Well, I don't want to miss my flight,' says Dad, tapping my shoulder. 'I'll see you Monday evening, hopefully not too late.'

'Yeah, see you then.'

Standing on the doorstep, I watch him climb into our car and drive away. I wait a few minutes, making sure he's not coming back, before I turn to my suitcase. Unzipping it, I look over the contents I packed yesterday. Grappling hooks, stethoscope, fake passport from previous heists, NVGs, pliers, torch, binoculars, change of clothes, dollars 'borrowed' from Dad's secret stash. I've taken such a small amount, he'll never notice . . . hopefully.

I think I've got everything.

The next hour is spent watching the clock. Come on, Ethan. How long does it take for a taxi to get from your school? At last a black cab rolls into our cul-de-sac and Ethan climbs out. He heads straight here before setting up his laptop on the kitchen table.

'Sorry I'm late. I had to see a teacher about something. But this is Delgado's place,' he says, tapping the computer. 'I hacked into your dad's files to get the address.'

An image of a large modern house made almost entirely of glass fills the screen. Balconies—the width of a room—run around the perimeter of each floor. The house is set in magnificent gardens with a tall wall surrounding the whole complex. But it's the wide strip of blue just inside the wall that I can't stop looking at.

'Is that a moat?' I say.

'I think so.'

'What sort of person has a moat?'

'The same sort of person who has security booths,' says Ethan, pointing to two boxes set in the wall on either side of the gate. 'At least that's what I think they are.'

'Can't you get any closer?'

He shakes his head. 'Because it's a really rural area, this is as close as Google gets. There's no street view either.' His fingers stroke the mouse pad and the camera moves to the right of the house. All I can see are fuzzy green islands. 'That's marshland. It goes on for miles and miles.' Then he scrolls back to the image of the house. 'I imagine the guards will be armed, there'll be cameras, and the house will be alarmed too.'

I frown at the computer. 'I guess my plan of scaling the walls and getting in through the skylight isn't going to work.'

'There is no skylight.'

'I realize that now. I'd come up with that plan before I saw this.'

'Lucky I've got an idea, then,' says Ethan, grinning. 'You transform into an eagle, fly over the moat, and go in by the chimney. You pick up Storm and the dagger in your talons.'

'And you mock me for my skylight! There is no

chimney. And do you honestly think I can carry a jaguar? Plus—', I slap him over the back of the head '—there's the small problem of me not being able to transform on demand. I have to be about to die.'

Ethan spikes up his hair again. 'You say that, but what about in the park? I don't think that pug was exactly life-threatening. And you were pretty safe in the taxi.'

'But I wasn't me. I was in the head of Storm and Storm's life was threatened.'

'Could you try to get in his head again when we're there?'

'I have no idea where I would even start with doing that.'

Ethan's grin drops.

Heads in hands, we both stare at the screen.

'Okaaaay', I say slowly. 'I think I've got it. You are going to find a blind spot in the cameras. I'll climb the wall using grappling hooks, making sure I'm not seen by the guards. Then I'll swim across the moat, enter the house, find the dagger, and rescue the jaguar.'

Ethan stares at me without blinking. 'That's your plan?'

'It's not exactly perfect.'

'No—perfect is not the word I'd use. But let's just say for some reason you manage to get over the wall, swim across the moat, get into the house, and find the dagger and jaguar, do you honestly think you can get them out again without being seen? Or, more importantly, eaten?'

CHAPTER EIGHTEEN

Trying not to think about the gaping holes in my plans, I drag my suitcase over to Ethan's.

'Sarah better be here soon,' says Ethan, unlocking the front door. 'We've got to leave before Gran comes home or Gran will make her tea and want to chat. We'll be stuck forever.'

Waiting in the lounge, we keep glancing at the clock. The TV, which his gran's addicted to, looks even more enormous close up.

'Sarah's always late,' mutters Ethan.

I start pacing the room and his foot taps up and down, when at last we hear the sound of a car. Through the window, I spot a green Mini Cooper pulling up, and I head into the hallway. Before the doorbell can ring, Ethan opens the door and a gasp escapes my lips. A girl of about twenty stands on the doorstep. She has the brightest pink hair I've ever seen and piercings in her eyebrow, nose, and lip. *This is his sister?* She blends into the background as much as a flamingo in the desert.

'Here,' says Sarah, holding out a large cardboard box.

'It came in time then. I was worried it wouldn't,' says Ethan, taking it from her.

'Anything for my little bro,' she says.

She reaches over to scruff his hair but he ducks expertly away.

'I called Gran about half an hour ago on her mobile,' continues Sarah. 'I told her how you're both coming to mine. She was absolutely fine with it.' She turns to look at me, her eyes running up and down. 'So . . . this is your girlfriend? Where are you taking her?'

Kill me now. No—kill Ethan now.

Forcing a smile to my face, I say, 'He's taking me to Paris to see my granddad.'

'Aww, how romantic.' She jangles the car keys. 'Are we ready to go? We don't have long.'

'Actually I need to do something first,' says Ethan. 'You'll be all right on your own?'

'I'm sure I'll live,' says Sarah, waltzing into the lounge. I peer round the open door to see her drop onto the sofa and grab a TV guide from the coffee table. 'But don't be too long. If Gran comes home, we'll never get away.'

I follow Ethan upstairs. As soon as his door closes, I say, 'I didn't think she'd look like that.'

'She doesn't wear piercings when Dad's around and

she's only just dyed her hair. It used to be blonde. Do you think I should send Dad a photo? Let him see the *real* her!'

'She's doing us a favour, remember?'

'Yeah. But not for nothing.' He tears open the cardboard box. 'I had this sent to my sister's, so school and Gran wouldn't know about it.'

Peering in, my breath hitches. There are bundles of wires, earpieces, a couple of turtle brooches—the shells brown and shiny. 'Is this what I think it is?'

'It depends what you think it is?'

'Mum used to use things like this for surveillance.'

'Then it's exactly what you think it is,' says Ethan, grinning. Then his face turns serious. 'When you were in that warehouse, I had no idea what was going on. And I felt so unnecessary. You were doing all these amazing things and I was . . . doing nothing.'

'That's not true. You were . . .' My words trail away.

'Exactly. So I thought I could help you more. That night, when I got back to school, I ordered these. The turtle brooch is a camera. When you wear it, it picks up images and sends them straight to my laptop. And when you speak, I'll be able to hear everything you say.'

'How can I see what you're seeing?'

'You can't. But you will be able to hear me through the earpiece when I speak into my turtle brooch.' He pulls each segment out of the box and lays it carefully on his bed. 'I need to calibrate them so they work with my laptop and we don't have much time. Can you be quiet for a bit? Or you can go downstairs with Sarah.'

'I'll stay here and be quiet.'

While he fiddles with wires, I wander over to his desk. There's a book on Aztec legends. Obviously Ethan's been doing research. Flicking through the pages, a symbol catches my eye. A rectangle covered in flames. Four diagonal sticks point from each corner into the middle. A cold chill waves through me, and although I don't know why, I feel as though this should mean something.

Underneath the drawing is a heading and some writing.

The New Fire Ceremony

In Aztec times, every fifty-two years the new fire ceremony had to be carried out or the sun would refuse to rise and the world would die. On the eve of the fifty-second year, every single fire in the land was extinguished. At sunset, a procession of priests would walk to the top of the highest mountain and sacrifice a man. They placed sticks on his chest and lit a new fire. If the sun then rose, the ritual had been a success. If not, then it had failed and every Aztec would turn on each other. They'd feast on each other's flesh.

Ugh!

The Aztecs sure liked sacrificing things! But as I look at the symbol again, I swallow hard. Why does it make me so uneasy? Then I snap the book shut. I have enough things to worry about without adding this to the list. Checking my watch, I see it 6:40. Ethan's gran is due back at seven.

'Are you done yet?' I ask.

'Just about.' He taps the keyboard a few more times,

then turns to me, smiling. 'It's all set up. You want to try them out?'

What a stupid question!

We pin the turtle brooch to our T-shirts and shove in the earpieces. Climbing onto the windowsill, I leap onto the tree.

'Whoa!' yells Ethan in my ear, and somehow I manage to cling on. 'This is mad. I can see the branches in front of you.'

'You don't have to shout,' I hiss. Then I leap from branch to branch until I'm on the ground.

'You're a freaking monkey.'

'Yeah? You're just a freak!'

I hurtle back up the tree and swing into his room.

'Do you think these will work when you're an animal?' he says, his eyes shining. 'You could be like my own personal animal cam.'

'I seriously doubt it. Everything I hold disappears.' I take out the earpiece. 'We should go now.'

'When we get downstairs, I'll distract Sarah. Can you put the surveillance equipment in your suitcase? It won't get past security in our hand luggage.'

But when we walk into the lounge, Ethan doesn't need to distract her. She isn't here.

'Oh God—where is she?' he says.

While he searches for Sarah, I stuff the surveillance kit into my luggage.

'Oh, come on! You can't take Gran's money.' Ethan's voice drifts through the walls. 'That's her savings.'

'I was just seeing how much she had. I wasn't going to take it,' says Sarah and I hear a drawer slamming shut. 'It *is* our inheritance.'

Ugh! Ethan's right—she is a nightmare. But we need her. And so I have a bland expression fixed to my face when they return to the lounge.

'We've got to go. Gran will be here any minute,' says Ethan, his face grim.

We hurry out of the house and pile into the Mini Cooper. Ethan and I are in the back, my suitcase on the passenger seat. I refuse to take my eyes off it. Who knows what Sarah might pinch?

The car squeals out of the cul-de-sac, wheels skidding.

'You know, we're trying *not* to attract attention,' says Ethan.

'Down,' yells Sarah. 'Gran.'

I glimpse the grey curls in a taxi and duck down. Ethan's head drops to his knees as well.

After a minute, Sarah says, 'You're safe now.'

She turns on the music and starts singing as Ethan and I sit up. He glares at the back of her head.

Trying to take his mind off killing his sister, I whisper, 'Where did you get the surveillance kit from?'

'The internet. But don't worry, no one will be able to trace the sale to us.'

'What about the plane tickets?'

Ethan's eyes shine. 'I hacked into one of the airport computers.'

I stare at him without blinking. 'You are turning into a master criminal.'

'Hey—I didn't steal them. I used your dad's money.'

'You did what?'

'Don't worry. He won't notice a thing.'

'I hope you're right because otherwise you and me—we're dead!'

The shine vanishes from Ethan's eyes.

After what seems like forever, I spot a large green sign for Heathrow. Suddenly I think of Dad. He's taking an aeroplane too. My blood chills. What if it's from Heathrow? What if his plane is delayed and I see him at the airport?

'Ethan,' I whisper. 'Do you know where Dad's flying from?'

'I don't even know where he's going. I've spent hours going through your dad's laptop but there's no sign of another heist.'

My nagging doubt spills over. 'Do you think Dad knows someone's looking at his laptop?'

'I've been worrying about that too, but I don't see how. I've been really careful. He can't know we're spying on him.'

I shudder. What kind of daughter spies on her own dad?

Sarah pulls into the drop-off zone at the airport. 'Remember our deal, Ethan?' she says, as I drag my suitcase off the passenger seat.

Watching her drive away, I say, 'What was the deal?'

'She helps us. I hack into the university computer and change her grades.'

'What?' I can hardly believe what I'm hearing.

'Hey—you're not the only one feeling bad about the dagger and Storm.'

107

CHAPTER NINETEEN

The airport is heaving. If Dad is here, we'll be really unlucky to see him. Saying that, if my last week is anything to go by, we'll bump into him any minute!

There's a long queue at check-in, but Ethan walks straight past it, to a desk for priority boarders.

'What are you doing?' I hiss.

'You'll see.'

The lady behind the desk frowns, before stretching her neck, peering round us as if expecting to see our parents. 'Are you alone?' she asks.

'Yes,' says Ethan, handing over our tickets, passports—his is real—and some paperwork needed for entry to America.

The lady keys in our details and looks even more surprised. 'You're travelling first class?'

I want to kill him all over again. Has Ethan honestly booked us into first class? Doesn't he realize we're under cover?

'I beg your pardon,' he says pompously. 'Mother never lets me travel any other way. Is there a problem? Shall I call her?' He pulls out his mobile phone. 'Can I take your name, please?'

The woman's mouth opens and closes. Her hand flies to her badge and I realize she's hiding it rather than showing us her name. Then she puts on a bright smile and says, 'There's no problem at all. I just want to make sure you're looked after if you're travelling alone.'

'We are more than capable of looking after ourselves,' says Ethan.

'I'm sure you are,' says the lady.

'We're being met at the other end, so there really isn't a problem,' he adds.

I hate to admit it—I'm impressed. I assumed Ethan would look nervous, guilty. But it's the lady's fingers that fumble as she wraps the destination tag onto my suitcase. I watch my luggage vanish down the conveyor belt. *Please don't lose it!*

Then Ethan and I make our way to airport security. I lower my head and let my hair fall over my face, when Ethan grabs my arm.

'You've got to act like we do this all the time. Stop looking like you're trying to hide or they'll think something's up,' he whispers. 'They're going to stare at us anyway. We're travelling on our own.'

I bite my lip. I know he's right—but when did he get to be in charge? I'm being demoted all over again. Taking a deep breath, I lift my head and hitch my rucksack onto my shoulder. Looking people straight in the eye, I march through security as if I own the place. No one questions me.

'Do you fly a lot?' I ask Ethan.

'Loads,' he says. 'The more confident and posh you are, the more likely they are to leave you alone. Sarah and I worked that out years ago.'

We make our way to Duty Free—a huge open-plan shop selling sweets, perfume, make-up, alcohol—when I hear a deep growl. I glance at Ethan but he doesn't seem to notice. Then there's an explosion of barking. This time Ethan stops and so do all the other passengers and staff. We look around, searching for the dog. Tell me it's not another pug.

'Must be a police sniffer dog,' says a lady from behind a beauty counter. 'Someone's going to be in trouble.'

'I've never heard it go mad like this before,' says her colleague.

The dog sounds like it's getting out of control. Snarls, barks. Probably frothing at the mouth. We hear pounding feet and a policewoman runs into Duty Free, a huge German shepherd dragging her in, straining on the leash. Wish it were a pug now.

'No one move,' she yells.

But people step away. Children start crying.

'Can it smell something?' I whisper to Ethan.

He shrugs. 'I don't know. Some dogs are trained to sense something out of the ordinary.'

My blood freezes. Ethan's face drops.

'Just in case—go,' he orders. 'Meet you at the departure gate.'

I inch backwards. Thank God people are between me and the dog. The handler doesn't know it's after me. Maybe it's not.

Clinging to that thought, I retreat even further. The barking gets wilder. Frenzied.

Someone screams, 'It's broken the lead!'

The words pierce my brain. I still don't know if it's after me but I'm not willing to find out. I twist and run. Travellers barge in all directions. I pummel the air with my fists and charge for the one place I always seem to find. The toilets. Bursting into the room, I see it's empty but the doors to the cubicles are all shut. I slam my fist against the first. It remains closed.

'Ooh, sorry, I'm in here,' someone calls.

I race down the line, banging each door. Occupants apologize but all I can concentrate on are the snarls and barks getting closer. Sweat drips down my back, my face. Two doors are left. I hit the first and to my utter relief it swings open. Leaping inside, I slide the bolt across.

Growls get louder. Claws scrabble across the ground, before scratching my door. Howling, the dog throws itself against the metal. There's no doubt about it—it's after me!

People scream either side of my cubicle. Thank God

there isn't a gap between the door and the floor. But looking up, I see a gap at the top. Can I climb over it? Will I fit?

'Teddy, Teddy!' yells a voice. 'Come here.'

The dog's called Teddy?

I climb onto the toilet lid.

'Back-up needed,' cries the same voice. 'Ladies' toilets by Duty Free.'

I feel dizzy, sick. I can't be found by the police. They'll look closer at my passport. They'll look at Dad . . . Balancing on tiptoes, I grasp for the top of the cubicle wall, when my wrist begins to tighten. I almost squeal with delight. Relishing the heat burning through me, I take deep breaths. My limbs and muscles melt. For a split second I wonder what I'll be. Then all thoughts disappear. My eyesight strengthens and I stretch out my wings, instinctively soaring through the narrow gap.

A dog barks wildly beneath me, saliva pouring from its jaws. A policewoman cranes her neck, her eyes almost popping out of her head. A black intercom slips through her fingers, crashing to the floor. I remember why I'm here, where I have to go.

Flying towards the exit, I squawk in outrage. Why are there always doors? I sweep round the room, just below the ceiling, out of reach. Then the door opens and policemen charge into the room. I soar above their heads, back into Duty Free. People squeal and mobile phones are jerked from pockets and bags. Too many signs and computer screens hang from the ceiling. I have to duck and swerve to miss them.

Suddenly a loud voice on the PA system announces, 'Flight number 57491 for Miami, your departure gate is now open. Please go to Gate 23.'

At least I know where to aim. Following signs for Gate 23, I swoop through the airport, far faster than the travelators below. Ignoring cameras and shrieking travellers, I reach the gate before the passengers do. Only the flight attendants are there, waiting for the crowds. Their eyes widen when they see me and they grab their intercoms.

I can't board the plane like this. I have to transform. But where? I need privacy.

I fly past more departure gates, hoping for one that's completely empty, when I hear a soft *phhht*. A dart shoots past, hitting the ceiling, crashing to the floor.

My heart slams against my ribcage. That was meant for me!

CHAPTER TWENTY

Twisting my head, I see three men with guns. I zoom in on their T-shirts. Bird Control Unit. I thought they were supposed to be outside the airport, stopping birds and planes from colliding.

'What are you doing?' I hear on old lady yelp.

'It's all right,' says one of the men. 'They're tranquillisers.'

That's all right, then!

Another man talks into his radio: 'The RSPB are on their way. Someone's smuggling exotic birds.'

A second dart whizzes past. Time to go! I soar as fast as I can, back through the airport. Come on—I just need one private space.

There are more and more calls for passengers to board the plane to Miami. And I seem to be flying further away.

Ethan must be going frantic. Then out of my side vision, I see an airport employee holding open a door for a businesswoman. I look through the doorway. The room on the other side is empty of people, but full of chrome and mirrored walls. Silently I glide over the businesswoman's head as she walks through the door. I perch on a chandelier. It sways and rattles but neither employee nor businesswoman look up. The door closes behind them and the noise of the airport vanishes. I watch them navigate the circular cream chairs and chrome tables. I feel like I'm in the lobby of an expensive hotel, not in the waiting room of an airport. I didn't know places like this existed.

'I would like to take a bath first,' says the businesswoman, as they disappear through a different door.

Without waiting another second, I fly over to the mirrored wall, my talons sinking into the soft gold carpet. I stare at my reflection and blink. I fit in here. I look grand and majestic. Regal. Then my feathers and wings retreat. My mousy hair, jeans, and scruffy rucksack reappear. I bite back a laugh. I'm definitely more acceptable as a bird.

Then suddenly I hear a squeak.

Spinning round, I see the airport employee from earlier. She looks . . . scared? My stomach drops. Did she see me transform?

We stare at each other, as if trying to work the other one out. Finally she walks towards me, her heels sinking into the carpet.

Forcing a smile onto her face, she says, 'Can I see your ticket, please.'

OK—I don't think she saw me transform. She's being far too calm.

'I don't have a ticket,' I say.

Her smile thins. 'This is an executive VIP lounge. You must have a ticket.'

'Sorry, I don't.'

Her smile drops completely. 'I knew you didn't belong in here. This is for first-class passengers on our airline only. Not—' she waves her hand up and down, her finger waggling '—the likes of you. I should never have left the front desk but we're short-staffed. Have any of my real clients seen you?'

Her eyes are full of undisguised disgust and bubbles of annoyance well up in me. Who does she think she is? Then Ethan's words come back to me and I stand up straight.

'Mother told me to wait in here while she's looking at Duty Free,' I say.

'What? I mean pardon?'

'Mother is looking at Duty Free. She told me to wait in here. She said I could have a bath if I wanted.'

Fear returns to the woman's face. 'Your mother told you that?'

'Yes. She must have my ticket.'

'Oh goodness . . . I . . . gosh, yes . . . she must do. Would you like a bath?'

'No. I would like to find my mother.'

I hoist my rucksack onto my shoulder and walk out of the room with my head held high. She scurries after me.

'We have lots of lovely different oils if you do want a bath. You don't need to find your mother just yet.'

I turn and look her straight in the eye. 'Yes, I do. We have lots to talk about.'

The woman's face pales.

'I will see you soon, no doubt,' I say.

I dart into the noisy crowds of passengers and burst out laughing. Ethan would be proud of me.

Then I hear: 'Last call for Miss Grace Hampton. Please go to Gate 23. Flight number 57491 is boarding.'

Grace Hampton—that's the name on my fake passport.

My laughter melts and panic rises. I hurtle through the airport, dodging other passengers, ignoring their complaints. It was easier being a bird, but at least I don't have to worry about being shot at. And thankfully there are no more sniffer dogs. I see the Bird Control Unit and the RSPB scouring the ceiling, but they don't look at me. My legs begin to ache and I get a stitch in my side but at last I reach Gate 23.

'She's here,' shouts Ethan.

'About time. Everyone else is on board,' says the lady behind the desk, her lips pursed. Ethan hands over our tickets and at last we board the plane. I try to ignore the glaring passengers and the mutters of: 'Where are their parents?' as I collapse into the large comfy seat.

I made it!

Ethan grins. 'So . . . even the dog knew you were a freak.'

My relief vanishes. His words cut through me like a knife.

'I don't believe it,' I whisper. 'Animals hate me now.'

'What? No!'

'They do. They hate me. I'm used to humans hating me or ignoring me. I can cope with that. But animals!'

'Scar, I was joking. They don't hate you. They might think you're strange, that's all.'

I glare at my wrist. 'Why did I ever put that stupid bracelet on?' Tears scratch my eyes and I swipe them away angrily. 'I think the bracelet's getting stronger. I'm transforming quicker and animals can see I'm getting weirder. That police dog wanted to kill me. The pug wanted to kill me.'

'Police dogs are trained to spot anything unusual. The pug was probably suffering form small dog syndrome. I'm sure most animals like you.'

'Your cat doesn't.'

'My cat doesn't like anyone, including me. You know that.'

I slump in my seat, feeling sick to the stomach. I was going to volunteer at Mum's old place of work, help get animals back into the wild. 'How can I help animals now?' I say.

Ethan takes my hand. 'You are here to help an animal. Think of Storm.'

I wrench my arm away, snapping, 'He'll hate me too.'

'No! He'll love you . . . for dinner!'

'You're not helping.' I sit in stroppy silence when an intercom beeps.

A voice fills the cabin. 'Ladies and Gentlemen, this is your captain speaking. I'm sorry to inform you but there is a mass of low-level fog heading our way. We won't be able to take off until it passes. Please do bear with us. We'll keep you informed at all times.'

What??? This can't be happening!

I turn to Ethan. 'Why can't they fly through fog?'

'I imagine it's health and safety.'

'Who cares about health and safety? We don't have enough time as it is.'

'We'll be all right,' he says. But as I look at his face, I know he's lying.

We're not the only passengers getting cross, but we might be the only ones not making a fuss, although I desperately want to. We're stuck in the airport as they chucked us off the plane hours ago. Apparently the fog has chosen to settle over the airport and is showing no signs of movement.

Checking my watch for the thousandth time, I clasp my head in my hands. 'It's seven in the morning,' I hiss.

'Don't forget Florida is five hours behind,' says Ethan.

'That's all right, then. We have all the time in the world.'

Sitting cross-legged, slumped against the wall, the image of the wooden room keeps returning. How long has Storm been trapped in there? I can still feel his panic, his fear. And what if we don't get to him by tomorrow night and he's sacrificed? It will be my fault. My eyes feel wet again, when suddenly I sit up straight.

Should I go to the police and tell them Delgado has the jaguar? I'll tell them I stole the dagger, keep Dad out of it. But . . . would the police even believe me? And Delgado might have someone else kill Storm just to get rid of the evidence.

I droop back down again. Then give myself a shake. This self-doubt isn't helping anyone.

I *can* do this.

I have to.

'You all right?' says Ethan.

I'm about to answer when a loud voice calls out over the PA system: 'Ladies and gentlemen, you'll be glad to know that the fog is finally lifting. Could all those people seated in first class please make their way to the departure gate.'

I leap to my feet. I just hope we're not too late.

CHAPTER TWENTY-ONE

We arrive at six o'clock in the evening, British time; one in the afternoon, Florida time. The sacrifice only hours away. I hate fog and health and safety!

It takes far too long to get off the plane, collect my suitcase, and go through security. I change as fast as I can and stand outside the men's toilets. I wait for Ethan. Come on! What are you doing in there? We've lost too much time already.

At last he emerges, looking perfectly groomed—buttoned short-sleeved shirt, tailored shorts. I wouldn't be at all surprised if he'd polished his trainers.

'Are you going to a wedding?' I say.

'Are you going to the tip?'

I look down at my tatty trainers, ripped shorts, and old T-shirt and shrug. Then, as I glance at him again, I

121

notice the freshly spiked hair. 'Did you bring hair gel?'

'Someone has to bring the important stuff.'

Shaking my head in disbelief, I walk out of the airport. The heat hits me straight away and I try not to think about scaling walls in this temperature. Swimming in the moat might be all right.

We head over to the first of a long line of yellow cabs outside our terminal. Ethan tells the driver our destination. A house near Delgado's—on the same road, but further along.

'That's quite a way,' says the driver, eyeing us suspiciously. 'It's at the other end of the Everglades.'

'My uncle lives there,' says Ethan, opening his bag, pulling out hundreds of dollar bills. I stare at it in astonishment. *Please tell me he didn't steal that from Dad.*

'My savings,' he mouths.

My insides groan. I'm not sure that's better. I'm going to have to find a way to repay him.

The driver puts my suitcase into the boot, then opens a back door. I climb in and want to squeal with joy. It's air-conditioned!

'First time you've been to the US?' asks the driver, taking us out of the airport.

As ever, Ethan is ridiculously polite, answering questions, asking questions. I sit in silence, looking out the window, wishing they'd shut up. We pass billboards, hotels, and apartments. But soon the scenery becomes more rural. Trees, marshlands, islands of long grasses. A canal runs parallel with the road, the only thing separating us from the wilderness. Apart from the odd tourist shop and airboat rental unit, it seems so primitive, unspoilt. I love it.

'Welcome to the Everglades,' says the driver. 'Nearly twelve hundred square miles of national park. Home to the alligators.'

I scan the marshy wetlands, hoping to see a reptile, but all I manage to do is make myself dizzy. At last I spot a sign saying Everglades Town and my lips dry. We're nearing Delgado's. The houses, hotels, and shops are all beautiful, low-level and pastel-coloured, but they seem strange after driving through wilderness. The taxi takes us to the other side of the town, and it becomes more rural again. Then we enter a long road where mansions hide behind massive hedges and walls.

Ethan nudges me. 'Delgado's,' he whispers.

I look out of his window to see a tall concrete wall obscuring the bottom half of a house. The top half is a sparkling rectangular block with walls made almost entirely out of glass, blackened so we can't see inside. Large open-plan balconies run round each floor.

We drive past the gate, the only gap in the wall, and I gasp. Ethan was right. These are security towers. But Google didn't capture the armed guards sitting in the booths. They're carrying machine guns. Is that even legal?

Ethan's face reflects my feelings. He looks horrified. We drive for a few more minutes, before the taxi pulls up beside another massive property. This one doesn't have armed guards or a towering wall. Why couldn't Delgado live here?

The driver whistles. 'So this is where your uncle lives?'

'He's a lawyer,' says Ethan, paying the man.

Clambering out, the smell of wet grass and salt from the sea drifts up my nose. The air is even hotter and more humid. By the time the driver puts my suitcase on the floor, my back is dripping with sweat. Ethan wipes his shiny forehead. We wait until the taxi disappears, before trudging back to Delgado's house. There are no pavements and we don't see another car. Arriving at the edge of Delgado's estate, the wall seems even higher now we're standing next to it.

'Can you see any cameras?' I ask, craning my neck.

Looking up, Ethan shakes his head. 'They might be at the top of the wall.'

We're too close to see the very top so we cross the road. Standing between two palm trees, we stare back.

'I still can't see any,' says Ethan.

'They could be on the inside.'

'I think we'd be able to see them. Normally cameras are positioned high up.'

I scratch the skin on my thumb. 'Doesn't this seem odd? They have armed guards in the security booths at the gate, but they don't have a camera or barbed wire or anything else.'

'They have a moat.'

'Yeah, but most people can swim. We're missing

something.' I look around and spot an enormous tree with branches dangling over the property wall. 'In a minute, I'm going to climb that, see if there's something else. But first, we need to get ready.'

Dragging my suitcase to a nearby bush, I crouch beside it and look around. I don't see any guards. Opening my suitcase, I transfer the hooks, stethoscope, lock pick, and all the other tools into my rucksack. I fix the brooch to my top and put the earpiece in, before turning to Ethan with his spy set. I stop and stare.

He's putting on sun cream. Then without looking at me, he pulls a small can out of his bag and showers himself with the most disgusting mothball-smelling spray.

'What *are* you doing?' I say.

'Getting ready.'

'Most people get ready with balaclavas or—I don't know—glass cutters, pliers.'

'Hey, you're the one going in. I'm not,' he says, spraying himself some more.

I scoot backwards. 'What is that stuff anyway?'

'Mosquito repellent. You should have some. We're in a swamp.' He holds out the can.

I shake me head. 'So let me be clear—you brought hair gel, sun cream, and insect repellent. Any swimming trunks?'

Ethan clasps his hands to his chest and squeals, 'Oh no! I forgot them!'

'Hah!' I hand him the turtle brooch and earpiece. As he puts them on, I pack his carry-on bag into my suitcase and shove the whole thing under the bush. 'Are you ready now? Or do you want to do your make-up?'

'I forgot that too,' squeals Ethan, his eyes shining, when a loud hiss comes from the direction of Delgado's house. 'What was that?' he yelps.

'I have no idea.' I gaze at the wall. 'Do you think it could be a security camera turning? A low one?'

Ethan shrugs.

Heaving my rucksack onto my back—it's pretty heavy now—I dart across the road to the overhanging tree. 'If someone comes, whistle.'

'What should I whistle?'

'I don't know! Anything.'

I snake up the trunk and creep along the branch as far as I dare. I lean forwards and peer over the wall. My hand slips. My pulse races. I grab for the branch and somehow manage to cling on. No wonder Delgado doesn't bother with extra security.

'Ethan, you are not going to believe this!'

CHAPTER TWENTY-TWO

'I can't see,' Ethan says in my ear.

I grab onto the branch again, stopping myself from falling. I forgot he was in my ear.

'All I can see is the wall. Your camera's too low,' he adds.

I stretch out my arms, lifting my top half higher, and Ethan whistles.

'Is someone coming?' I squeal, flattening myself to the branch.

'No! Sorry! I just saw alligators.'

I breathe again and lift my body so both of us can stare at the large reptiles lying motionless in the water. Dark green, almost black, frozen prehistoric beings.

The moat is about ten metres wide, dug deep into the ground. Smooth steep walls stop anything inside from

127

escaping. There are small marshy islands with shallow waters leading to deeper waters filled with fish and weeds. Some of the alligators lie half on, half off the small islands.

'What kind of person uses this as security?' I say.

'I wish he had barbed wire now.'

Without taking my eyes off one particularly large creature gliding majestically through the water, I mutter, 'Perhaps I could get in through the main gate?' I'm talking more to myself than to Ethan, but he replies with a yelp, 'You can't. There are armed guards.'

'Only two. How many alligators are there? There's no way I can jump over the moat—it's too big. And funnily enough, I'm not swimming.'

'Scar, hide!' hisses Ethan.

I duck down, as two men in black suits, dark glasses, earpieces, and machine guns appear from behind the house. They saunter around the balcony, about fifteen metres away. *Please say the leaves are covering me.* I stay as still and silent as the alligators until the men disappear behind the building again.

'They might be doing circuits. They could be back any minute,' says Ethan.

'Oh great!' I whisper. 'This is useless.'

'No, it's not. You haven't tried becoming an eagle yet.'

'It won't work. I have to be about to die.'

'At least give it a go!' he says sharply.

He's right, of course. 'OK, I'm going to try,' I whisper. I close my eyes and imagine my wrist tightening, my body warming. I think about soaring through the sky. Nothing happens. *Don't give up*, I tell myself. I think about the jaguar locked in a small room, afraid, alone. I feel the anger rise through me. I clench my fists, but my wrist remains free.

'I told you it wouldn't work,' I snap.

Ethan curses.

I glare at the house. We're so close . . . but so far. 'I can't let Storm die.' My voice breaks and I clear my throat quickly.

'I'm coming up,' says Ethan.

'What?'

'I'm coming up.'

I look down to see Ethan clasp a bough in his hands. His legs scrabble at the trunk. It's like watching a baby giraffe climb a tree. I don't think I've ever seen anyone so uncoordinated. If I wasn't feeling so frustrated, I'm sure I'd be laughing now. At last he scrambles onto the branch next to mine.

'Didn't you ever climb trees when you were younger?' I ask.

He peers over the wall, his face ashen. 'We're really high,' he croaks.

'I didn't ask you to come up.'

'I know.' He looks back at me. 'We don't have much time, do we?'

'No. The sacrifice is tonight.'

'I'm really sorry, Scar.'

'Why? It's not your fault Delgado's a nutter who keeps alligators for security. '

Ethan squirms forward on the branch, past me. Soon

he hangs over the water, over the alligators. Has he taken brave pills? Or stupid pills?

'Get back,' I say.

'I think there's a narrower part of the moat. You might be able to jump it.'

'Really?' I shift forward. The bough buckles as I reach him on a parallel branch. 'Where?'

'I really am sorry.'

'For whaaaaa . . .'

His hands shove my sides and suddenly I'm falling.

'You'll be an eagle!' he cries.

Frantically, I grab for the tree, but my fingers scrape through air. I'm heading straight for the edge of an island. More importantly, the alligators. My heart thrashes. Then, to my utter relief, my wrist strangles, my body warms . . . but I'm not rising into the air. I'm plummeting. I crash straight into the shallow water, my body slapping the sandy bottom. I smell oil and salt. As my brain tries to compute what's happening, I realize my eyesight, my hearing, my smell are so much stronger.

I lie half submerged on the island, motionless. It feels so natural to let the world move around me. Then slowly I become aware I'm drifting off the island into deeper water. Hearing a gasp, I look up. A boy hangs onto a branch. Ethan.

My brain catches up.

I'm a freakin' alligator!

CHAPTER TWENTY-THREE

I start to thrash the water with my stumpy limbs. Spray flies everywhere and my body shoots downwards. Nooooo! I need to be above the surface. A layer of film clamps over my eyes. I open my mouth, gasping for breath, but water pours inside. Can I drown? Is that even possible? I thrash even more. My tail hits the wall and burns. Wait—I have a tail? Of course I have a tail.

OK—I need to calm down.

I force my limbs to stop moving and my body stills. I drift under water and suddenly realize I don't need to breathe. I have enough air in me. Slowly I move my tail and glide gracefully, majestically. My limbs float behind. Long grass tickles my skin. A leaf from a tree above drops onto the water and I feel the ripples rebounding off my scales.

Gradually, I resurface and the layer of film flicks backwards off my eyes. I look around. Smooth, steep walls tower over me.

My gut twists. I'm trapped. How the hell am I going to get to Storm? To the dagger?

Then I feel a rush of ripples. Something is getting closer. I don't have to be a genius to guess what. Without a second thought, I dive into deeper water, waving my tail harder.

That's when I see it.

In the wall on the side of Delgado's house is a gate—a row of iron railings—half submerged under the moat. There's a tunnel behind it, which surely goes under Delgado's house. And if there's a tunnel, there must be a way out.

I swim straight for the gate. I want to grab a railing with my teeth, rip it out, but my snout won't fit between the bars. Argh! I turn around and spin at speed, my tail whacking it. The bars don't budge but my skin stings. Of course—it has to be alligator-proof.

I duck to the bottom to see if there's a gap. I'm not surprised when there isn't. But as I rise, I spot a lever at the top of the gate.

Swirling back onto my stomach, I grab onto the railings with my claws and scramble upwards as if climbing a rope ladder. I stretch my body as far as it will go and the tip of my snout just reaches the lever. Clamping my teeth around it, I let gravity and my body weight pull down hard.

The screeching of iron against stone hurts my ears, but I don't care. I swoop under the opening gate into the tunnel and swim. But soon the ground slopes upward and the water becomes shallower. My clawed feet scrape cement and it's impossible to swim.

I turn a bend and plunge straight into darkness. If there was a glimmer of light, my eyes would catch it, but there's only blackness. Blindly, I slap along the steepening slope. The water disappears completely and my body grows cold. I feel stiff, sluggish. I can't seize up here. Forcing myself to move on, I turn another bend.

There's a glint of sunlight. Instantly I can see much better and I scrape the ground faster. As the tunnel warms, my body feels more alive. And then I hear a hiss. Another alligator must be following.

I scrabble frantically to the end of the tunnel, but to my horror find another set of iron gates barring my way. Looking up, I spot the lever is on the other side. How can I get through? Then I see the gaps between the railings are further apart. Using my tail as a leg-up, I stretch upwards and shove my face between the bars. They scrape my skin, burning my scales. But when I hear the alligator's claws getting closer, I bulldoze harder. Finally I hit the lever. The screeching starts and the railings disappear into the ceiling above.

A ramp lies in front of me. I sprint across it and soon find myself on the ground floor patio, Delgado's house behind, the moat in front. I must have crawled under the whole complex.

A ferocious hiss pours out of the tunnel.

With a burst of terrified energy, I lift onto my claws and turn a corner. I freeze. Two armed guards—one tall, one short—block my path. Their eyes widen.

'How did you get out?' yells the taller man.

He points his machine gun to the sky and releases a barrage of bullets. He's not trying to hit me. They're warning shots. Then I hear claws scratching the ground again.

'There's another one,' shouts the shorter man. 'A giant.'

My legs go weak. I feel light-headed, sick. There's an alligator behind me, armed guards in front. I'm trapped. The taller man fires again. This time, the shorter man lifts his arms and I realize they're trying to herd us back to the moat. I can't go back in there. I need a way out.

My eyes flicker right and my heart stops. I'm staring into the dark glass of Delgado's house at a scaly green reptile. And that scaly green reptile is me! Seeing it seems more shocking than being it. The skin round my left leg tightens. My body heats—not because of the sun this time. My scales begin to bubble. There's no way I can transform into a girl now. Not in front of those men and certainly not in front of a giant alligator.

CHAPTER TWENTY-FOUR

I could run for the house but they'll follow or, worse, shoot me. Plus I can't see an open door. My mind spins. I look back at the other alligator. He *is* enormous. I shudder to think what he'll do to me if I'm a girl.

Then it comes to me. A plan—or should I say death wish? I have to get the timing right or I'm dead. I scoot over to the edge of the moat.

'That's right, in you go,' says the shorter man. 'And you too, big fella.'

Giant's feet scrape the ground. He's following me. Oh well—if I die, at least I'll have saved his life. They won't kill him if he jumps.

I leap onto my claws. Instead of dropping over the side, I run along the edge of the wall. One of the men curses. He starts to chase me but I sprint even faster. My muscles are melting rapidly, the scales disappearing.

It's now or never.

I jump over the edge of the moat just as my body fully transforms. My rucksack reappears on my back.

'Scar! I have visual again,' Ethan shrieks in my ear. My heart almost bursts out of my mouth but somehow I remain focused. Pirouetting in mid-air, I face the wall and grab onto the edge. My fingers cling to the rim. Jerking my head left, I see Giant leap too. His body slams into an alligator below and the two start tearing flesh out of each other.

I grip the edge even tighter, the front of my body draped against the wall. Sweat drips down my back. My feet dangle a metre above the top of the water. Can alligators jump? Then, metres away from me, the two men appear at the edge of the moat.

'Whoa! Easy, boys,' says the shorter man.

They're staring at Giant, but if they turn their heads, there's no way I won't be seen. My fingers turn white. My muscles scream. But I can't move. Silently I thank Dad for all his training.

'Scar, where are you? All I can see is a beige wall,' says Ethan in my ear.

I stare at the men. *Can they hear him? Will they turn this way?* But they remain fixed on the alligators.

'Scar, can you hear me?' says Ethan.

Yes, but I can't answer you!

'Scar, Scar, can you hear me? Is everything OK?' He's getting louder and louder.

If I could, I'd rip out the earpiece and throw it to the alligators.

The shorter guard leans further forward. 'You gonna tell Delgado about this? That the gators got up here?'

'I don't think there's any need. What he don't know, can't hurt him,' says the taller guard.

'Scar, I'm coming in,' says Ethan.

No! I want to scream.

'I'll go to the gate, tell the guards you're in there and . . . oh, I don't know. Please answer!' He sounds more and more desperate..

The men gaze at the writhing alligators. They seem mesmerized. My body grows heavier. Ethan's voice more frantic. *Just move!* I can't hold on much longer.

'How do you reckon they got up here?' asks the taller guard.

'No idea. Let's check the gate.'

One of my fingers slips and I grab for the edge again. My feet hit the wall, making a soft thud. Have the guards noticed? But when they turn round, it's not in my direction. They start to walk away and soon their conversation and footsteps fade from view.

Finally!

'Ethan, I'm in the compound,' I whisper. 'I'm all right. Don't leave your post. I can't talk now.'

Using all of my strength, I pull my body higher. My fingers burn but at last my chest hits the rim. I release my fingers from the edge, letting my arms take the weight. My hands are stuck in claw-like positions as I elbow the patio floor, dragging the rest of my body over the top. Rolling away from the edge, I lie for a moment, staring up at the cloudless sky. That was too close.

'Where are you?' says Ethan.

'By the moat, trying to—you know—catch my breath.'

'Have you checked for cameras?'

I sit bolt upright and look around. Phew—there are none. I guess Ethan was right. Delgado doesn't think anyone will cross his moat. I can't stay here, though. The guards might come back at any moment. Or even Delgado himself.

Clambering to my feet, I stretch out my arms. My fingers click as I uncurl them. Tiptoeing over to the glass wall, I try to peer through. The glass is dark and reflective, so I've no idea what's on the other side. For all I know, hundreds of armed guards are looking at me right now, ready to shoot me down. Or, as it's Delgado's house, maybe there are reptiles like Komodo dragons or pythons waiting to attack. Normal people have guard dogs!

There has to be a door here somewhere. Creeping along the side of the house, I spot a sliding door in one of the glass walls. I take my gloves from my rucksack and wince in pain as I squeeze my fingers inside. I can't leave prints. Then I take out the lock pick. But when I look, there doesn't seem to be a keyhole. There's no sign of an alarm either.

'Ethan, am I being really stupid? Can you see a lock anywhere?'

'I'm looking. Move about a bit.'

I sway in front of the door.

'Nope. I can't see one,' says Ethan.

'What about an alarm?'

'I'm crossing my fingers for you.'

I take a deep breath and slide the door an inch. Silence.

'Delgado trusts his guards,' I whisper.

'Or they're too scared of him to do anything.'

'I prefer to think the first.'

I thrust the door further along its rails and slip into the room, the air conditioning hitting me like an iceberg. Luckily, there's no one inside, not even a reptile. Well . . . no one living. My hand flies to my mouth. Not that smell again. I bend over, clutching my stomach.

'Scar, are you OK?'

I can't believe my eyes. Looking down, I'm almost frozen in shock. I'm standing on a rug made from a South China tiger. Is Delgado trying to wipe out the entire species single-handed? I leap off it. No animal deserves to be stood on. Especially a magnificent beast like this.

I hear Ethan curse. He must have seen it too.

'I feel sick,' I whisper.

'It's OK, you can do this.' He pauses. 'Just take deep breaths.'

'I can't take deep breaths. I'm inhaling death.'

'All right. Then I need you to concentrate. Can you hear anyone in the house?'

I want to kick myself. Normally that would be the

first thing I checked when breaking and entering. I listen out for a creak or a whisper.

'It's silent,' I say.

'OK. That's good. Now Delgado told your dad the dagger was for a plinth. Can you see one anywhere?'

I shake my dizzy head, trying to clear it. Then turn around slowly. The room has modern minimalist furniture in it. No stone stand anywhere. Nor a dagger.

'Go to another room,' instructs Ethan. Something in his voice makes me obey.

I stagger into a hallway and take deep breaths, hoping for fresh air. But I inhale rotting flesh. Swallowing back saliva, I stare in horror at the Amur leopard-skin encased in glass. There are only hundreds left in the wild. Minus one.

'Any sign of a plinth?' asks Ethan.

I look around and shake my head.

'Is there any sign of a plinth?' he repeats.

Of course, he can't see my shake. 'No,' I gasp and hurtle through another door into a study. A stuffed red parrot perches on a desk. A scarlet macaw. The smell is overwhelming. I lean back my head and hurl. The dinner from the aeroplane splatters to the ground.

'OK . . .' says Ethan. 'I think they'll work out someone's been here.'

'I couldn't help it,' I mutter.

'Don't worry about it. I don't blame you at all.'

Now that I've actually been sick, I feel better, more focused. I know I don't have much time. The guards might appear at any moment. I return to the hallway, flinging open different doors, searching for plinths and daggers, when I spy a set of steps leading to a steel door. My heart pounds. Racing down, I turn the handle, expecting the door to open. It doesn't. My heart pounds even more. This is the first room that's been locked.

'The dagger must be in there,' says Ethan.

'Just what I was thinking.'

Putting my pick in the keyhole, the cogs turn. The door swings open and a light flickers on automatically.

'Wait!' shouts Ethan. 'What if the jaguar's in there?'

I stare into the room, clutching the wall to stop myself from falling.

CHAPTER TWENTY-FIVE

Floor-to-ceiling glass cabinets line the walls. Rifles, shotguns, pistols, bullets of different sizes, bows, and arrows fill the shelves.

'At least he keeps them locked up,' says Ethan.

'That's all right, then. He only takes them out when he's planning to kill!'

'Is there any sign of the dagger or plinth?'

I don't want to go inside. It feels wrong but I force my legs forward. I circle the room, hurrying past weapon after weapon. 'They're all modern,' I say, darting back outside, locking the door. 'Why does he need so many?'

'He's a collector,' says Ethan.

'Couldn't he collect stamps?'

Ethan chuckles as I climb up the stairs back into the

hallway. Fighting through the smell, I rush up to the next floor. At last I can breathe easy. There's no death up here. I fling open doors and find bedrooms and bathrooms, but I can't see a plinth. I just hope he hasn't put the dagger in a safe.

The next floor is the same and soon I run out of stairs. There's only one door on this landing. Without hope, I push it open to find a massive room with a four-poster bed. Unlike the others, this room feels lived in and I bet it's Delgado's bedroom. Somehow this feels more intrusive than searching the rest of the house. Stepping inside, a whimper escapes my lips. Tucked in an alcove stands a stone plinth, waist height, covered in Aztec engraving. There's nothing on top of it. My heart feels like it's being crushed.

'He must have the dagger with him,' I whisper, moving the camera in front of the stand. 'What should I do now? Ethan? Ethan?' I tap my turtle brooch and earpiece. 'Ethan, can you hear me? Ethan!'

Suddenly I hear his voice. High-pitched, trembling.

'I'm sorry, sir. I was just climbing a tree . . . owwwww! No. Please, sir . . . I'm here on my own . . .'

NOOOO! Ethan's been caught!

Without a second thought, I charge down the stairs. The smell of death flies up my nose. Through the earpiece, I hear Ethan's yelps and groans. *What are they doing to him?* My legs get faster and faster. My wrist tightens. *Please let me be a jaguar, not an alligator.* But as I jump down the remaining staircase, I glimpse the Amur leopard-skin hanging on the wall. My reflection in the glass screams back at me. My wrist loosens.

Not now!!!!

I leap over the tiger rug and hurtle out the front door straight into the back of a guard. The heat blasts into me. The guard spins around, his gun flying in my direction. I don't know who looks more startled—him or me?

'Don't move!' he yells in a deep drawling voice. 'Put your hands where I can see them.'

I shove my arms into the air.

My heart starts pounding and my body heats, but I can't transform in front of him. I look straight into his aviator glasses and see my terrified reflection.

'What are you doing here?' he says, his eyes falling to my bag. Within seconds it's ripped off my shoulder.

Oh God!!!

Tearing it open, his eyes widen. He pulls out the grappling hooks, the stethoscope. 'You're a thief?'

'A cat burglar,' I croak.

'Are you alone?'

I don't have time to answer. Five guards appear from round the side of the house. In between two of them is a boy looking down. They're dragging him by the armpits and the tips of his trainers scrape the ground.

'Are there any more of you?' demands the guard I crashed into.

'Just us,' I say.

'Check the house, check the grounds,' he says and two of the guards disappear through the door I came through.

Turning to me, he adds, 'You better not be lying.' He pulls out a radio and darts round the side of the house, leaving Ethan and me alone with the other three. I'm guessing he's the boss.

'You OK?' I say to Ethan.

'Shut it!' yells one of the guards, aiming his machine gun at me.

Ethan lifts his head. His right eye darkens with every second and blood drips from his mouth.

How dare they? My wrist tightens and I grit my teeth. I will transform—I don't care who sees.

The Boss reappears from around the corner. 'Listen up,' he barks, hoisting my rucksack higher onto his shoulder. 'I've called Delgado. He wants us to bring them to the cabin straight away.'

The cabin. Four wooden walls. I stare into his aviator sunglasses again.

CHAPTER TWENTY-SIX

Guns poke our backs as we're led through the house. Trying not to inhale the stench of carcasses, I shiver uncontrollably. I don't know whether it's from fear or from the air conditioning. Ethan's face, where it isn't bruised, is turning greener, and I wish I could grab his hand.

The two guards from earlier run towards us. 'Can't find any more of them,' says one. 'These must be the only two.'

The Boss nods and escorts us down the steps to the steel door. We're going to the gunroom? I thought we were going to the cabin. He unlocks the door and we're shoved inside. The guns seem to taunt me even more.

The Boss strides over to the corner of the room and bends down. He pulls on a large metal ring on the floor and heaves a thick square of wood to one side. A trapdoor. How could I have missed that? I'd been in such a hurry. If only I'd looked down . . .

'In,' says the Boss, jerking his gun at me.

Forcing my feet to move, I walk over to the square. Steep stairs lead to a pit of darkness. Taking a deep breath, I step onto the first. Lights flicker on automatically and now I can see that the stairs seem to go on forever.

'Hurry,' says the Boss.

I climb down and down, hearing the feet of Ethan and the guards behind. At last I reach the bottom step and enter a long narrow corridor. The Boss overtakes me, and leads us though the stark white hall. We must be going under the house, under the moat even. I try not to think about how many layers of concrete or gallons of water are pressing down on us. Then the corridor starts sloping upwards until we reach a door at the other end. There's an electronic keypad beside it and the Boss enters a code. In a way I feel a bit better. Even if I'd found the trapdoor and the corridor, I wouldn't have been able to work out the exit code.

The door opens.

A gun pushes even harder into my back and I stumble into fresh air. My feet land on a wooden platform. An airboat floats just in front of us, and behind that is marshland and mangroves. The Everglades.

Turning my head, I see a giant wall and the top of the back of Delgado's house. I was right—we did walk under the entire complex.

I feel a hand grip my shoulder and I'm shoved towards the airboat. It's about the size of a large pick-up truck with an enormous caged propeller at the back. There are three rows of seats. The first two are low down, but the back two seats are elevated, about my head height.

'You're next to me,' drawls the Boss, pointing to one of the raised seats at the back.

I climb on board and the boat wobbles a little. Ethan's escorted into a seat at the very front and three more guards fill the remaining chairs. Reaching into his pocket, Ethan pulls something out.

'Get your hands where I can see them,' snaps the Boss, jerking his gun.

'It's my inhaler,' yelps Ethan, his arm freezing in mid-air.

The Boss gives him a look of pure disgust. 'Use it.'

I watch Ethan take a big gulp and my insides churn. I shouldn't have brought him here. I guilt-tripped him into it. Tears stab my eyes and I turn away.

The sun is setting over the Everglades. The sky burns red, the water still, like liquid steel. Clusters of mangroves jut out in little islands and the smell of warm salt drifts towards me. I hear the honk of a bird and look up to see a dot soaring in the sky above. At any other time I'd be impressed.

'Fifty minutes and we'll be there,' says the Boss.

My stomach flutters. Fifty minutes and we'll be with Storm.

The boss turns the key in the control panel situated

between us. The propellers start spinning. Against the quiet still air, the noise is deafening. Water churns and waves of ripples crash the calm. He stamps the one pedal at his feet and the airboat starts moving. The breeze feels amazing on my skin.

'How do you stop this thing?' I say. 'There's no brake.'

'Take your foot off the accelerator and drift to a stop.' Then he turns to me, his brow furrowing. 'You sound like you know how to drive.'

'I watch people,' I say. Oh God—I have to keep my mouth shut. I don't want to give anything else away.

'You from England?' he says accusingly.

There's no point in lying. 'Yeah.'

He doesn't say anything else and his face is a blank mask. He grips the long lever next to him and pushes it forward, manoeuvring the airboat right.

We head through a tunnel of trees and I can't believe my eyes. Bright green mangroves stick out from the water. Their brown roots above sea level, twisting and turning in all directions. Some clusters are surrounded by golden sand, making them actual islands. The water changes from blue to green to blue again. Something long, dark green, prehistoric moves towards us.

'Is that a wild alligator?' I squeal.

'Don't think about jumping overboard and swimming away. You might not get far,' says the Boss with a cruel laugh.

I tear my eyes away from the giant reptile and glance

at Ethan. Although he keeps checking his watch, his back is rigid.

'How are you holding up?' I whisper into the brooch.

'I want to be sick.'

'Aim on the guard if you can.'

His shoulders lift up and down in a laugh and I smile to myself.

We navigate the network of islands as the sky darkens. Bright stars fill the sky and the moon looks like a magnificent glowing ball. Perfectly round . . .

My blood freezes. It's already up in the sky.

'Are we nearly there?' I ask.

The Boss smirks.

The airboat powers through another mangrove tunnel. Then the Boss takes his foot off the accelerator. Straight ahead, illuminated by moonlight, is a log cabin. It's half hidden by trees on an island of golden sand. We pull up behind another airboat tethered to the side.

'Everyone out,' says the Boss.

I change my mind. I don't want to help Storm. Delgado can keep the dagger.

This cabin is steeped in evil.

CHAPTER TWENTY-SEVEN

I watch Ethan climb off the airboat but I don't move.

'He said, everybody out,' growls a guard from the front.

I stumble out of the boat and the ground seems to wobble even more. We're standing on another floating wooden platform. Ethan's hand slips into mine, and he clasps my fingers. I thought I'd be reassuring him. I can't believe how loud it is. Frogs and whatever else is out there seem to be making as much noise as the airboat did.

Suddenly there's a yelp. Without realizing, I squeezed Ethan's hand too hard.

'Sorry,' I whisper, letting go.

We follow the Boss across the sand, towards the cabin. He lifts his hand to knock on the door but it whisks open before he connects with the wood. Candlelight flickers in the background.

We freeze.

Delgado stands in the doorway dressed in a jaguar headdress, a cropped tunic, and a loincloth. The trees in the moonlight cast shadows over his face. He looks like a warrior. Sinister. Grand. Fit for a deadly ceremony. He steps out of the cabin, his eyes flickering between me and Ethan.

'So these are the thieves,' he says, his voice low and commanding.

I gulp. Delgado seems to be completely different from the person I saw outside the warehouse. It's like he's channelling some ancient Aztec spirit. He steps closer to me. I tense my muscles, fighting the urge to leap back. I don't want to show him I'm scared.

'Why were you in my house?' he asks.

'This will give you a clue,' says the Boss, throwing my rucksack towards Delgado.

The contents clank as Delgado catches it. He unzips my bag and looks me straight in the eyes, as if trying to delve into my brain. 'What exactly were you after?'

I swallow. I can't tell him. It might make him suspect Dad.

Leaning forward, he whispers in my ear, 'I asked you a question.'

I start to shake.

Delgado straightens up again and nods to the Boss. The Boss jabs the end of a machine gun at my temple.

'The dagger,' blurts Ethan.

What? I glare at him, warning him to say nothing more.

'The Dagger of Eztli. We know you have it,' cries Ethan.

Astonishment flashes across Delgado's face. But it disappears so quickly, I'm not entirely convinced I saw it. 'How do you know about the Dagger of Eztli?' he asks.

I watch Ethan gulp as he realizes his mistake. The gun moves swiftly from my head to his, when all of a sudden, we hear a growl. A jaguar.

Storm is in there!

Delgado twists around. 'Bring them into the cabin,' he commands, striding inside.

Guns prod our backs. Although every fibre in my body tells me not to step into that room, I have to see Storm for myself. I take a deep breath and walk inside, the guards following closely behind. The cabin is just as I saw it in my visions—except now a green velvet fabric drapes across one wall. And a beautiful white jaguar lies on the large stone altar.

Storm!

He lifts his head and opens his eyes. They're vacant, confused. A dart flies into his side. He growls once before crashing back down to the altar.

My head jerks round to see Delgado holding a large revolver.

'The last dart,' says Delgado grimly.

Has he killed him? But surely he needs to use the

dagger. Looking back, I see Storm's chest rise up and down. He's been drugged again. His tongue lolls out and he looks so undignified. This is wrong.

Then an icy coldness hits my core.

Delgado is letting us see the jaguar, which must mean one thing: Delgado's planning to kill us too. There's no way he can afford to let witnesses go.

I feel my body heat rise and my wrist tighten. About time. I couldn't care less who sees it happen. I take a deep breath, relishing the heat, but the smoke from the candles seems to swirl into my lungs. I cough and the feeling round my wrist loosens. What the—?

Surely now, more than ever, is a life-threatening situation.

Then I realize Delgado is staring at me curiously.

'That's a leopard!' I cry. 'What's a leopard doing here?'

Ethan looks at me in wonder. *Come on, Ethan. We can't act as though we expected this!* I wish I'd thought to tell him earlier.

Then Ethan's eyes widen. 'Is it dead?' he yelps.

Yes—he's got it!

'It's a jaguar. And it's not dead . . . yet,' says Delgado, with a leer I want to scratch off his face. 'But it will be.'

'Why?' I demand. Even though I know the answer, I want Delgado to tell me.

He lifts his arms into the air. 'So it can become my Nahualli, my animal spirit. It will guide me through my life. It will help me with my hunts. It will be worthy of me.' The last words come out in a scream.

You're sick! Demonic! How the hell am I going to get us all out of here?

I stare around the room. There, on the altar beside the jaguar, lies the Dagger of Eztli and a goblet for the blood. Is he going to use those on us too? My stomach twists and flames of anger build up inside of me. But my wrist refuses to do anything. What's happening? Bracelet, don't fail me now.

Delgado strides over to the altar. 'Let the ceremony begin,' he says, picking up the dagger.

The room vanishes. Everything goes black.

CHAPTER TWENTY-EIGHT

I feel at peace. So calm. I could lie here all day.

Oh hell! I'm in the jaguar's head again. And he's sleeping. All I can see are the insides of his eyelids. Then the darkness vanishes and I'm back in the cabin. Delgado's eyes are closed, his arms outstretched. The dagger is on the altar again. What is going on? What caused that vision?

I gasp for breath as Delgado starts spinning around. Then he picks up the dagger . . .

And the world goes black. My breathing deepens. Storm and I are like one, melded together. Then the wooden walls and the guards return.

I stare at the dagger now lying on the altar. It's when Delgado touches it!

The candles flicker. Shadows sweep through the cabin. Delgado looks even more godlike, as if this is his destiny.

He picks up a candle and lights four pots of liquid. The sickly sweet smell of burning pine forests wafts towards me. Then he brushes his finger around the top of the goblet and lays the same hand over Storm's heart.

Why won't I transform? I glare at my wrist. Then squeeze it with it my other hand, trying to kick-start it into action. But all I can do is watch.

'Why aren't you transforming?' whispers Ethan.

I shrug helplessly.

Delgado stares at each of us in turn, his hand still on the jaguar's fur. 'Like the Maasai Mara warriors of Kenya, I can kill a wildcat with only a dagger.'

'They don't drug the lions first. They battle them,' I spit.

Delgado's lip pulls back in a snarl. His fingers clench the fur over Storm's heart. I need to do something but the smoke seems to be swirling all around me, suffocating me. There aren't that many candles or incense in here. What's going on?

He starts chanting. Nahuatl, the language of the Aztecs, I'm sure. He reaches for the dagger, but I can't have everything go black again.

'You can't choose your own Nahualli. It's impossible!' I scream.

Delgado stops. Then turns to me, flames reflecting in his eyes. 'You dare tell me about Nahuallis. I am descended from the Aztecs. '

'But a true Aztec would never kill an animal to get one. You're mad,' I cry.

His face reddens, his nostrils flare. Suddenly I feel arms wrapped around me. Someone's tugging me away.

'She's ruining the ceremony,' says the Boss. 'Let me take her outside.'

'No.' I squirm frantically, but he tightens his grip.

'Do you want to die?' he hisses in my ear.

'Throw her to the alligators,' says Delgado.

The Boss whisks open the door and fresh air swoops inside, and for a second my wrist burns. But then smoke fills my lungs again. I glance at the flames and the trickles of smoke. My heart starts pounding. Could smoke be the reason? Is that why I can't transform? I stop struggling and allow myself to be shoved through the doorway.

'Get on the airboat. The raised seat,' whispers the Boss, before dumping me on the sand.

The last thing I see is Ethan's terrified face before the door shuts. I take deep breaths and cool, fresh air fills my lungs. Delgado's chants get louder. My wrist tightens and heat rushes through me. Finally. But I don't have much time. He'll be picking up the dagger any second. I yank off my trainer and throw it to the ground.

Spreading out my arms, I relish the melt. Closing my eyes, I pray, 'Let me be a jaguar to terrify Delgado.'

Then I hear soft ripples of water and open my eyes. I'm low to the ground. I turn around, my stomach sweeping over the sand. The water beckons. I want to sink below it, feel it cover my scales. Then I hear chanting. Nahuatl. Ancient words I understand.

'God of the fate of mortals, god of the night sky, help me

release the spirit of the wildcat. I will drink its blood until its spirit lives within me. Let the jaguar be my Nahualli. Let it guide me, hunt for me. Let it die for me . . .'

Forgetting about the water, I wheel back round. Ready to burst through the door, I charge, when I spot my trainer. Carefully, I grasp it in my teeth, the laces dangling out of my mouth. Then I slam my tail against the door. The cabin shakes.

Ethan yells. The chanting stops.

'What was that?' asks a guard, the terror in his voice unmistakable.

'The blessing of the gods,' shouts Delgado. He chants again, louder, more frantic. 'I sacrifice the jaguar in the name of—'

Using all of my strength, I fling my tail against the door again. This time it crashes open. Lurching onto my claws, I run straight into the cabin. Screams hit the walls.

'That's her trainer!' yells Ethan.

I try to wink at him. I think I grimace, but I see his lips twitch.

'It ate the girl!' shrieks a guard, plastering himself against the back wall.

'It saved me the trouble of killing her,' yells Delgado. 'Now nobody move. I *will* finish this ceremony.'

He picks up the dagger and I freeze, waiting for the cabin to disappear, waiting for everything to go black. But the four walls remain. Delgado, the guards, Ethan—I can see them all. Is it possible the link between Storm and me breaks when I shape-shift?

Delgado lifts the dagger into the air and holds it high above Storm's heart. He shouts in Nahuatl, 'For you, the gods, I sacrifice this jaguar.'

The dagger plunges towards the jaguar's fur. Spinning as fast as I can, my tail whacks the base of the altar. Pain shoots up my body but the stone leg crumples. The table tips. As if in slow motion Storm slips down the stone surface, landing in a heap at the bottom.

'My Nahualli!' shrieks Delgado, rushing towards the wildcat.

I swing again, my tail connecting with Delgado. He falls backwards dropping the dagger. Candles tip over. Flames lick the wooden walls and the green fabric is set alight. Fire and smoke fill the cabin.

'Get the dagger!' screams Delgado, scrambling across the floor.

Charging after him, my feet slap the burning ground. Ethan lurches across the room too, and I watch his fingers clasp the dagger. He shoves it into the back of his shorts.

Three guards aim their machine guns at him.

'It's not worth it. Give them the dagger!' I shout, but only a hiss comes out.

Ethan stands paralysed in shock.

'Kill him!' shrieks Delgado.

CHAPTER TWENTY-NINE

I spin round, my tail connecting with the three guards. They topple like dominoes. For a split second, I almost laugh. Then I see their bodies tumble into the flames. *NO!!!* They can't burn. Do I have to drag them out of the cabin?

Then I see the Boss race towards them. Yanking two of them to their feet, he throws them through the open door. The third guard tries to stand.

'Delgado, help!' he cries, his shirt on fire.

But Delgado doesn't appear. Twisting round, I see him in the corner of the room, his hands around Ethan's neck. Squeezing. He looks like the devil. Eyes stinging from smoke, I hurtle across the burning floor. My jaws clamp Delgado's leg and he crashes to the ground.

The walls blacken. The roof shakes. Searing heat surrounds me.

'Ethan, get out!' I cry, but he can't understand.

Suddenly the Boss is back, no longer wearing a shirt. He's wrapped it around his mouth and nose. He grabs the third guard and throws him outside. 'Roll on the ground,' he shouts, before rushing back in. He whisks Delgado into his arms, cradling him like a baby. Blood drips from the bitten leg. Smoke whips up from the grey-black hair. Is he on fire?

Delgado screams, 'The dagger!'

The Boss looks at Ethan. 'Come on, boy. I'll help you.'

'No,' says Ethan, backing into the fiery corner. 'I'm not leaving the jaguar.'

The roof creaks again and the walls tremble. The Boss races into fresh air with Delgado in his arms, as an airboat engine roars to life.

I look Ethan straight in the eyes. *Go!*

This time he seems to understand. He races past me and makes it outside.

Now I know he's safe, I dive back into the centre of the burning cabin. I grasp the middle of Storm's body with my teeth and drag it across the scorching floor. The wooden walls shrivel. The flames shoot up the doorway. There's no other way out.

I take a deep breath of smoky air and run as fast as I can. With fire burning my scales, I burst through the doorway onto the sand. I want to stop, want to collapse, but I smell singed fur. Forcing my legs on, I reach the edge of the island and dive into the mixture of salt and fresh water. My body instantly cools. I could stay here forever but the jaguar needs land. I clamber back onto the sand and lie down. The cabin withers away before my eyes.

'Scar, you need to get Storm on the boat,' cries Ethan. 'Who knows if the fire will spread?'

I turn to see him in a raised seat on the second air-boat. Delgado, the Boss, and the guards must have left on the other one. My stomach churns as I think of their burning shirts. *Please say they're OK.* I pick up the jaguar again and claw my way over to the boat. I throw him onto the first row of low seats. He lies half on, half off, his chest heaving up and down.

I climb onto the airboat too and wait for the engine to start.

Nothing.

'We have to tie him up, just in case he wakes,' says Ethan. 'You have to change back.'

All I want to do is lie down—no, all I want to do is slink into the water—but the flames are getting closer. Luckily, the smoke is pouring the other way. I peer over the edge of the airboat. Ancient yellow eyes with slitted pupils look back at me. And slowly but surely, my dark scaly skin begins to bubble. My hair and clothes reappear. Ugh—they're cold and wet. I'm cold and wet.

I clamber to my feet and the boat wobbles.

'What can we use?' I ask, looking around.

'I found rope,' says Ethan, holding out a long thick red twine. 'It feels as though it's got metal inside. Storm shouldn't be able to bite through it if he wakes.'

163

'Wrap it around his feet.'

Ethan steps backwards, shaking his head. 'He's your kindred spirit. Not mine.'

Seriously?

'I'll tie the other end to the side of a seat,' he adds.

Taking the rope from him, I slowly creep towards the sleeping beast. Storm doesn't even twitch. Carefully, I wrap the twine around his ankles. I pull tight, cringing as the rope snags against his skin. 'This is for your own good,' I whisper. 'I don't want you jumping out of the boat.'

Ethan ties the other end to the chair and soon we're both sitting in the high-up seats in the airboat. I turn the key in the ignition and the propeller starts. Then I stamp my foot on the accelerator. Pain shoots through me. My foot is burning but I have to keep pressing. I grip the steering stick and push it forwards, driving us straight onto sand.

'Wrong way. Heading towards fire!' shrieks Ethan.

'I know,' I snap, yanking the steering stick the other way. The airboat turns the way I want.

'Straighten up!' shouts Ethan.

'I'm trying,' I say, jiggling the steering stick. The Boss made it look so easy.

We inch forwards off the island and at last hit water. I pull the steering stick backwards and the airboat moves left. OK, I am getting the hang of this. Slowly. We drift away. When I look back, the flames are licking the mangrove trees. Some of the branches are overhanging another island. 'It won't spread it, will it?'

'It should stay on the island. The water should contain it,' says Ethan, lifting his hand. His fingers are crossed.

I cross mine too, then look up to the sky and whisper, 'Aztec gods, if you are out there, don't let the fire spread.'

I look back but nothing happens. I'm not sure what I expected—a clap of thunder? A rainstorm?

'I think you have to sacrifice something,' says Ethan.

'Are you volunteering?'

'There's a drugged-up jaguar and I got the dagger.'

I burst out laughing, the tension draining away from my body and Ethan joins in.

'I can't believe you did it,' he says finally.

'*We* did it,' I correct. 'And at this rate, we'll get Storm to safety and still make it to the airport on time.'

We fall silent. The only sounds—burning trees, the propeller and very loud singing frogs. We drive through a mangrove tunnel, passing a narrow island. A long dark shadow slinks off the sand into the water. Eyes reflecting the moonlight head straight for us.

Ethan yelps.

'We're OK. We're on an airboat,' I say, trying to sound braver than I feel. It was one thing being amongst alligators when I was one. But now . . .

I put my foot further down on the accelerator and wince. But better a hurt foot than alligator food. The mangroves loom above us, and I feel like we're getting deeper and deeper into a maze. We twist and turn down the narrow waterways and soon reach a fork in the swamp. Oh God. We must have come this way but I've no idea which way to go. It's the middle of the night and we're lost.

CHAPTER THIRTY

Ethan stands up and holds his right arm out in front of him. He turns around on the spot.

'Watch it,' I snap. 'You're making the boat wobble. And you know what's out there.'

'You need to go that way,' he says, pointing towards the right fork.

'How do you know?'

'Because my watch has a compass. I brought it especially.'

'You did?'

Ethan's eyes twinkle in the moonlight. 'Unlike some, I'm always prepared. We headed south-east from Delgado's house—I kept checking. So to get back we should go north-west.'

I turn the airboat. 'Sometimes you really surprise me.'

'I also got your bag,' he says, lifting it into the air.

I forgot about that! I think I might actually want to hug him, when something bites my arm. I slap my skin, but the mosquito's darted off already. Looking into the moonlight, I see hundreds if not thousands of the creatures swarming around us.

'As you're always prepared, I don't suppose you still have your spray?' I say, as another mosquito lands on my leg. I slap it quickly, this time getting it. *Yes!!!*

'Of course I do.' He pulls a small canister out of his pocket and sprays himself before adding, 'Tell me you weren't trying to kill that mosquito. I thought all creatures deserve to live.'

'I was giving it a warning,' I say stiffly, hoping Ethan can't see the squashed creature stuck to my thigh.

'Here,' he says, shoving the can in my hand. 'So you can *warn* them some more.'

Spraying all visible skin, my stomach twists. I killed that creature without a second thought. Am I just as bad as Delgado? Or a meat eater? From now on, I won't kill another mosquito. I don't care how much they bite me.

'I'm putting the Dagger of Eztli into your bag,' says Ethan. 'You'll be able to keep it safe.'

'You were amazing, risking your life for it. Thank you.'

Ethan shrugs, but even in the moonlight I can see his cheeks turning pink with pride. I watch him place the dagger carefully into my rucksack.

'You don't get visions when you touch it?' I say.

'No. I'm not the freak among us.'

We swoop through the endless swamp, trying to ignore the long shadows that appear silently. Soon we come to the back of Delgado's house. My body grows cold and numb, but luckily no one is on the dock. I push my foot all the way down. Clocking 45 miles per hour, I speed past the house and all the other mansions in billionaires' row. We hit open water and I see lights twinkle from buildings in Everglades Town.

'Where to now?' I ask Ethan.

'I don't know.'

'What do you mean you don't know?'

'How on earth am I supposed to know where to take a drugged-up jaguar?'

'But you have a compass.'

'Yeah—it points north. Not to the drugged-up jaguar zoo.'

'OK, OK,' I say to myself more than to him. 'We can park the boat somewhere in Everglades Town and call animal welfare.'

Then Ethan's face drops. 'Did you see that?'

'See what?'

He points at Storm. The jaguar twitches.

'Oh no,' I whisper. There's a soft groan.

'Tell me he's not waking up!' yelps Ethan.

'He's not waking up!'

'Do you really mean that?'

It's difficult to breathe, let alone talk. But I manage to croak, 'Nope! He's waking up!'

CHAPTER THIRTY-ONE

We stare in horror at the twitching beast. I try to put my foot even further to the ground but the boat is already going as fast as it can.

'You're going to have to park it now,' yelps Ethan.

'I can't. Storm's still drugged. He can't fight an alligator. We need the main town.'

'Then get there quickly.'

'He's tied up.'

'Yeah. But how long is the rope?'

I look at the coils of red rope lying on the base of the boat. Argh! We've given him far too much. He could easily reach us.

Ethan and I don't talk as we hurtle through the open water. The lights get closer and we see what type of buildings there are.

'We could take him to the police station,' says Ethan.

'I wish. If the police see a jaguar, they might shoot it. I can't take that risk.'

'What about a boathouse? There's one there.'

I look to where Ethan is pointing. We could easily slip the boat inside. But I shake my head. 'The owners could have guns too. They're legal in the US.'

'What are you planning to do, then?' shouts Ethan.

'Stop shouting!' I shout.

My legs weaken. Storm growls softly, baring his teeth. But he lowers his head again and looks dazed. A dazed and confused jaguar or an alert jaguar? I'm not sure which is worse. Ethan's body starts to tremble.

'Try not to show fear. Animals smell fear,' I whisper, but my body starts shaking too.

I feel dizzy, my heart racing. At least there's no smoke—I should be able to transform. But . . . what about Ethan? Then I check my wrist. It's not being strangled. It's doing nothing. *I hate this bracelet!!!*

Then I see a sign splashed across a building and I know exactly what to do. Thrusting the steering stick left, the boat swerves, tipping on its side. Water sprays over the top.

'Watch it!' yells Ethan.

Without slowing down, the airboat heads straight for the grass.

'We're going to crash!' he cries.

'Hold on!'

The rubber bottom hits the grass and we fly into the

air. It slams back down, but still doesn't stop. We bump and slide across the grass. Ethan yells. Storm growls. And even I can't stop the screams coming from my mouth. The building with the neon yellow light looms in front of us. I take my foot off the accelerator and the boat slows down. We come to a stop near the entrance.

'Are you trying to kill us?' demands Ethan, still clinging to the boat, even though we're going nowhere.

Then I see a door open and a silhouette of a person dart outside.

'Quick.' I grab Ethan by the shoulder and throw him out the back of the boat. I'm about to jump too, when I hear a low rumble.

I turn to see Storm, his head up. We look each other straight in the eyes. Straight into each other's souls.

'You'll be safe now,' I whisper.

His left ear twitches.

'Your welcome,' I mouth before leaping over the side, joining Ethan on the grass.

We half stumble, half run towards a set of trees. Storm growls, louder this time, and I watch the person halt. Then I see him running back to the building.

'He might be going for a gun,' says Ethan.

'Please say it's a tranquilizer. That's the animal hospital. I saw the sign.' I lean back against the trunk. 'They must be used to alligators. A jaguar's not that different.'

'You do know one's a reptile, the other's a mammal.'

'I meant they're both potentially dangerous,' I snap, as Storm decides to roar again.

I peer around the tree to see the man jogging back towards the airboat, a gun in his hands. A woman runs beside him.

Please, please be a tranquilizer. If Storm is killed now, after all we've done, I don't know what I'll do.

A shot rips through the night sky. My body stiffens. The air seems too thick to breathe.

CHAPTER THIRTY-TWO

The woman creeps closer. 'Call Zoo Miami now. I know who that is.' Her voice rings out loud and clear.

Yes!!!

Ethan and I grab onto each other and squeeze . . . before I shove him away.

'How he did he get here? Who brought him?' asks the man.

'Let's go,' I whisper.

We dart through the trees towards the main part of town. It's busier and louder than I would have thought. Bars are open, with music blaring and people drinking. We keep to the shadows.

'How are we going to get back to the airport?' says Ethan.

'I have a plan,' I say, heading round the back of a bar into a car park.

I take my gloves out of my bag and stare at the rows of cars. Pick-up trucks, 4 × 4s, old bangers. Which one to choose?

The back door to the bar opens and a man stumbles out. Ethan and I duck down between two parked cars. Peeking out, I watch the man sway from side to side, his body knocking car after car. Luckily, none are alarmed. He fumbles in his pocket before pulling out a key.

'There's no way he should drive,' whispers Ethan.

'My thoughts exactly.'

The man lurches towards an old blue banger. He presses the key fob then gropes for the door handle. Missing, he lurches forward again.

'I think we have our ride,' I say, standing up.

'I'm not getting in the car with him. He'll kill us.'

'Not if he's the passenger.'

I walk calmly towards the man, the smell of liquor hitting me metres away.

'Hi there, let me take that,' I say, grabbing the key out of his hand.

'Eh? Who . . . wha . . . who?'

'I'm your driver. You called me. You wanted me to take you home.'

'I . . . did?' He falls against the car and slumps to the ground.

'Yeah. You knew you were going to have too much to drink.' I grab the handle and open a door in the back.

He collapses onto the seat and I close the door on his feet, ignoring his yelp. Then I look over at Ethan. 'Quick, before someone comes.'

We climb into the front and I pull the seat as close to the dashboard as I can.

Ethan looks over his shoulder, his nose wrinkling. 'He stinks. Where are we dropping him off?'

'We're not. He's coming to the airport with us.'

I start to head out of Everglades Town. Snores rumble from the backseat—I can't believe he's fallen asleep already—when Ethan sits up. 'Your suitcase,' he says.

My jaw clenches. I'd love to leave it behind but Ethan's laptop is in there—with all of Dad's information on it.

My hands grow clammy and Ethan puffs on his inhaler as I drive back to the road where Delgado lives. Thankfully, we don't have to go as far as the main gate and we don't see any security guards. More importantly, they don't see us.

Ethan jumps out and darts under a bush, while I keep the engine running. Seconds later, he returns, lugging my suitcase. He shoves it into the boot and I start to drive again.

'What time do we check in?' I ask.

'Ten in the morning. Not for a while yet.' He pauses. 'I can't believe we managed to get the dagger back and save Storm so quickly.'

We turn to each other and grin. It's as though it hits us both at the same time—what we've managed to do.

'We are epic!' I shout.

'Huh?' groans the man in the back.

Slamming our hands over our mouths, we snort with laughter.

Then Ethan turns to me. 'Scar, do you ever wish your dad knew about the stuff you could do? Your transformations? How you rescued a jaguar?'

I grip the steering wheel. 'I would love him to know. Sometimes I have to stop myself from telling him.' I hesitate. 'I'm guessing you wish your dad knew about you too. He'd be proud.'

'That's the thing—he would be. But I can't tell him. He thinks I'm just this geek who doesn't do anything but play on a computer.'

'Well, thank God you are a geek. Without your skills, none of this would have happened. I wouldn't have even been able to get to Florida.'

'Thanks,' says Ethan quietly.

I take the Tamiami Trail back to Miami. It's one seemingly endless straight road and before long, my mind and body grow tired. Plus the drunk isn't the only one snoring now. Ethan's drooling and making the strangest of noises. Maybe I should film him on his phone and send it to his fans . . .

As soon as I hit Miami, though, the ease of the one road vanishes, replaced by a maze of motorways, swooping under and over each other like some sort of wacky roller coaster. The roads are busy even though it's three in the morning. I try to follow signs for the airport, but the car lights are dazzling, hypnotizing.

My eyelids feel like cement is weighing them down. I've been up for so long. I'm so glad I'm now in bed. . .

BEEEEEEEEP

My eyes flash open. We're swerving into another lane. Someone's slamming their horn.

CHAPTER
THIRTY-THREE

My heart thrashes, trying to escape my chest, the car. *OH MY GOD!!!* I fell asleep. I yank the steering wheel as Ethan sits bolt upright.

'What happened?' he splutters.

'I need some sleep.' I stretch my eyes as wide as they'll go.

'You want to pull over?'

'I'm not sleeping in the car with him. We need a motel.'

Ethan looks over his shoulder and jumps a little. 'I forgot about him.'

I drive into the car park of the first motel I see. Cheap and run-down. Where staff are unlikely to ask questions.

'What about our passenger?' says Ethan.

'He can sleep it off in the car. We won't be long—I

just need a few hours. Then we can go to the airport. He'll probably still be sleeping.' *I hope . . .*

I lock the car and pocket the keys, leaving the man snoring in the back. I grab the suitcase and together we make for reception. The girl behind the counter doesn't look much older than me. Using the money I took from Dad, I pay her in cash. She yawns and continues reading her magazine. Soon Ethan and I are in a small room with twin beds. Without bothering to speak, I collapse onto the nearest. I think I fall asleep before I even hit the duvet.

'Scar, wake up!' Ethan is prodding my shoulder. 'Our plane is in an hour. We haven't checked in.'

I try to open my eyes but they seem glued shut. 'What time is it?'

'Nine.'

I scramble out of bed, grabbing my bags. 'Is the man still in the car? Is he sleeping?'

Ethan shrugs.

We rush outside. The car's still in the same place—after all, I have the keys—but there's no sign of the drunk.

'He must be close by,' I say, looking around.

Ethan rests his hand on the bonnet. 'Do you think we can *borrow* his car for a little bit longer? Take it to the airport? Or is that too mean?'

'It might teach him not to get drunk,' I say, when I spot a large pick-up truck parked metres away.

I gaze at the gold lettering plastered across its back. My mouth dries. Golden Glades Island Resort.

Ethan turns to see what I'm looking at and his eyes widen. 'Oh no. Tell me you're not thinking what I think you're thinking.'

'That's where the fashion show is, isn't it?'

Ethan doesn't reply.

'What time does it start?'

'The same time our plane takes off.'

I can't tear my eyes away from the truck. I was so happy last night at everything we achieved . . . but we haven't stopped Delgado. He could still hunt more animals. 'For all we know, he'll try to sacrifice another jaguar,' I say out loud.

'We've got the dagger,' says Ethan.

'He could use something else.'

'I thought the dagger was the whole point. We need to get it away from him. Not let him get near it again.'

My gut tightens. Ethan's right. If we go to the fashion show and he catches us, the dagger will be his.

Ethan stands in front of me. 'Scarlet, we can't worry about this now. We have to get to the airport. You can't be late for school. I can't be late for school.'

He's using my full name!

'Don't you think stopping Delgado is more important than school?' I ask.

'But what can we do?'

Ethan looks so pleading . . . and I think about everything he's already done for me. I can't expect him to do more.

The words taste sour as I force them out. 'You're

right. We wouldn't be able to spoil the show anyway. You keep a look out for the drunk while I unlock the car.'

His face fills with relief. I almost feel better. Then a man wearing smart white overalls with the words 'Golden Glades Island Resort' walks past us, a coffee and doughnut in his hands. I try not to watch him climb into the pick-up truck.

Ethan's eyes dart between the man and me. He starts spiking his hair.

'Oh, I'm going to regret this,' he whispers.

'Regret what?'

'Scar, get in the pick-up truck. I have an idea.'

CHAPTER THIRTY-FOUR

Crouching low, I scoot over to the back of the pick-up truck. The driver climbs into the front seat, sipping his coffee, eating his doughnut. Taking a deep breath, I scramble over the side, squeezing myself between a lawn mower and a strimmer. My eyes dart to the back window of the cab. I don't think the driver's seen me.

My rucksacks digs into my back and I squirm a little. Then my body goes weak. The suitcase. I left it in the motel. Do we have time to get it? I lean over the edge, as Ethan grabs onto the side of the truck.

'My suitcase,' I hiss.

Ethan curses and drops back down. 'I'll go.'

He takes two steps when the engine fires up.

Noooo!

Ethan turns to look at me. Do I jump out too? Then

I think of the furs, especially the South China tiger. And I think of Delgado's smug face.

'Forget the suitcase,' I whisper.

'My laptop.'

'We'll get it later. The room is locked.'

Ethan looks torn, but he grabs the ledge and heaves himself over. I grab his arm, yanking hard. The truck moves as his body slams inside. If I were the driver, I'd notice the bump. I wait for the truck to stop, for the driver to investigate, but it keeps on going.

'I can't believe we left your bag,' says Ethan, lying next to me.

'Forget about it—there's nothing we can do. Tell me what your idea is.'

The ride is bumpy, loud, uncomfortable, and my suitcase stranded at the motel is at the back of my mind, but as Ethan shouts his plans in my ear, I can't help but grin.

'It's so simple, it's genius,' I say.

He beams proudly.

'Unless . . . this truck isn't going to Golden Glades. It's just been there,' I add suddenly.

His face falls. 'I hadn't thought of that.'

We lie in silence, bumping along. *Please stop soon. Golden Glades isn't that far away.* Looking at Ethan's face, I know he's thinking the same. The truck begins to slow. I lift onto my elbows and peer out. *Yes!* We're on the causeway—the road built to join mainland Miami to the island. No other cars are behind us, so I crawl onto my hands and knees. Leaning out to see what's happening ahead, I duck back down again. We're at a barrier and a guard is walking straight towards the cab.

'Alfonso, you know you have to show ID,' drawls the guard.

'How many times do I come here?' says the driver, who I assume to be Alfonso. His voice is thick with a Latin American accent.

'Rules are rules. I value my job. Show me ID and I lift the barrier,' says the guard.

'Fine. It's here somewhere.'

Through the window into the cab, I see him rummaging around.

'I can't find it. Come on, let me in,' says Alfonso.

'Rules are rules,' says the guard.

My jaw clenches. *We're so close. Should I help him look?*

'Got it!' says Alfonso finally.

The truck starts and my muscles release. We move more slowly this time and don't bounce about as much. From my position amongst the cargo, I see the tops of palm trees and glistening roofs of villas. After about three minutes of twisting and turning, the truck stops. Now comes the difficult part. We have to get out before Alfonso comes round the back, and we have no idea who else is out there.

I peep over the top. We're parked beside a row of villas. Exotic flowers fill the individual gardens. I can't see anyone, so I hop out. Ethan tumbles out. Then together we hurry to the back of the nearest villa.

'We should pretend to be guests. Act confident like back at the airport,' says Ethan. He fiddles with his hair and smooths down the wrinkles in his shirt.

Even though Ethan's slept in his clothes, he looks well dressed. Peering down, I realize I look like I've been evicted from a rubbish dump. I try to comb my hair with my hand, but my fingers get lost in knots. Maybe the other guests will think I'm a rich, eccentric type.

'We need to find out where the fashion show is being held,' I say.

Strolling out from behind the villa, as if we belong, we see the man who brought us here. He unloads the lawnmower and pays us no attention. Trying not to feel self-conscious, I walk beside Ethan. We pass beautiful pastel-coloured buildings, but nothing big enough to house a fashion show. Gardeners, cleaners, and many other people dressed in immaculate uniforms smile politely and say hello. Well . . . they smile at Ethan. They look at me in surprise.

I stop next to a woman searching for something in her cleaning cart. 'Excuse me. Could you tell us where the fashion show is, please?'

She shakes her head and looks apologetic. 'I sorry. No speak *Inglés*.'

'*Hola*,' says Ethan, stepping forward. '*Dónde está el desfile de moda, por favor?*'

Whoa! I stare at Ethan in shock.

The woman beams. '*Sigue la calle hasta el final. Gire a la izquierda. Es un edificio a la derecha.*'

'*Muchas gracias*,' says Ethan. Then he turns to me. 'We have to follow this road all the way to the end, then turn left and it's a building on the right.'

'You speak Spanish?'

'Yeah—they teach it at school.'

'They teach it at my school too. Doesn't mean I learn it,' I say.

We walk for what seems like forever—past villas, swimming pools, restaurants, bars, valet parking. It's so hot. I think I might disappear in a puddle of sweat. At last we hear different accents, different languages, and the clink of glasses. Turning a corner, we stop. Men in suits and women draped in gold and diamonds are standing in front of a sprawling building. They're chatting, laughing, drinking from champagne flutes. Fans fill the air with a fine cold mist.

'You stay here. I'll see if there's a way in round the back,' I say, when a large hand clamps my shoulder.

I swallow my scream.

CHAPTER THIRTY-FIVE

Ethan yelps. I turn my head. A guard dressed identically to those outside Delgado's house holds onto Ethan's shoulder too.

'What are you two doing here?' he says.

'We're going to the fashion show,' I say, wriggling to get out of his grip. It doesn't work.

My words seem to knock the fear out of Ethan. 'Our parents are invited and they won't be pleased to learn we're being manhandled,' he says, sounding important.

'Oh, really?' says the guard, squeezing our shoulders tighter. 'Because I didn't think kids were invited. This is an adult-only resort.'

You're kidding? An island without kids. Why would anyone want that?

'Yes . . . but . . . our parents are such great friends

with the Delgados, we're allowed to be here,' says Ethan.

'Why don't we find Delgado just to make sure?' says the guard.

Oh God!

My wrist tightens, my body warms. The skin on my hand starts bubbling. I pull away and twist at the same time. My bones liquefy. Slipping out of the guard's grip, I hurtle over the hedge into the back garden of the nearest villa. Paws hit the ground instead of feet.

I hear the sound of running and heavy breathing. Someone's chasing me. My natural instinct is to bolt. Halfway past the figure-of-eight swimming pool, I hear a scuffle. Looking over my shoulder, I see a guard jump the hedge. I recognize him and somewhere inside my brain a voice shouts, *You have to stop him.*

Stop him from what, I do not know. And right now I do not care.

Twisting around, I race towards him. He halts, paralysed in shock. I smell his uncertainty, his fear. A delicious mixture. I pounce, pushing him backwards. My jaw stretches round his scalp. My teeth scrape his head.

'Scar! No!' yells a voice.

I freeze.

'Don't do it.'

Feet appear in front of me. I look up and see Ethan shaking his head violently. 'Don't kill him!'

I step backwards. There are tiny dots of blood in

the guard's hair where my fangs bit. He's trembling and breathing fast. Too fast.

Ethan crouches down straight away. 'Are you all right?' he asks the guard.

The guard's breathing slows down. Good—he's not going to have a heart attack.

'What is that?' he whispers, heaving onto his elbows. His eyes flicker between me and Ethan.

'It's my pet,' says Ethan.

Pet???

'My parents aren't really here. My friend and I just used that as an excuse,' he continues. 'Delgado asked us to bring our wildcats for the show. He told us not to tell anyone.'

'*That* is yours?' says the guard, his eyebrows shooting to the top of his head.

'Yeah,' says Ethan.

'You can control it?'

'Yeah,' says Ethan again. 'I'll show you. Scar, lie down.'

Oh no, you don't!

'Scar, lie down,' he repeats, sharper this time. 'We're part of a circus. She's young and sometimes finds it hard to obey.'

I want to scratch out his eyeballs. But I know what he's doing. And so with claws extended, I lie down.

'Good kitty cat,' says Ethan.

I growl, *Don't push it!* And Ethan swallows.

'Where's your friend?' asks the guard.

'She's gone to get the tiger. Do you want to see him too?'

'No, no. I have other things to do,' says the guard quickly. 'I think you should get yourself into the main building before someone gets hurt. There's a door round the back. Key in 7936 and you're in.'

CHAPTER THIRTY-SIX

I lie in the shadows of the auditorium next to Ethan who is standing. We came through the back door, and he told everyone we met that we're part of the show. No one—the models, the make-up artists, the hotel employees—seemed that surprised. What kind of holiday resort is this?

So now we're positioned in an alcove, hidden from everyone. From here, there's a great view of the stage lying at one end of the room and the catwalk running down the middle. The guests from outside have filled the purple velvet seats. Their gold and diamonds glint in the light from the chandeliers, and the place stinks of perfume.

The room turns dark. A spotlight appears on stage.

'This is it,' whispers Ethan, pulling out his mobile phone.

Delgado walks down the catwalk, dressed in a tuxedo. He looks different . . . it's his hair. He has none! He must have shaved off the bits that didn't burn.

Delgado surveys the audience with the most self-satisfied grin I have ever seen. I step forward, wanting to rip it from his face, when I feel a hand on my fur. Actually touching my fur. I whisk around, baring my teeth. Ethan trembles, but shakes his head.

'You have to let the fashion show start,' he whispers.

Argh! He's right. I slink back into the shadows.

'Ladies and gentlemen from all over the world, I welcome you to our exclusive fashion show,' says Delgado. 'My wife, Melinda, has worked incredibly hard to ensure the most beautiful clothes have been created. Each unique, not only in design, but material too. No tiger has the same stripe, no leopard has the same spot, so neither will you.'

The audience bursts into spontaneous applause.

I want to dig my claws into his heart. That's if he has one . . .

Ethan grips my fur even tighter, as if he knows what I want to do.

'My wife,' says Delgado, stretching out his arms. 'In Sumatran tiger.'

A woman draped in a striped fur dress shimmies onto the stage. The audience gasp and clap furiously.

I fight back the roar building in the back of my throat.

'I am so pleased to see many of my old friends, and I can't wait to make new ones,' says Melinda. She has an

English accent. For some reason I expected her to be American. 'But I know you don't want to hear or look at my husband and me. You want to see my new collection. However, I have a couple of things I must say first. If ever questioned about your purchases today, you must never give our names. And you must never wear any of my designs out in public in the UK or the USA. Oh—and no photos, please.' Her voice is sweet but the undertones of ice are unmistakable. She waves her hand in the air. 'Enough of the silly business. You will see many delights today but the final outfit is really my *pièce de résistance*. We will be auctioning off the South China tiger cape at the end. It might just be the only one ever made . . . unless my husband can find another one. Now let's get on with the show.'

I didn't think I could hate anyone more than Anton Delgado, but watching Melinda makes me change my mind.

They disappear offstage and the music begins— something classical with violins and oboes. A model glides onto the catwalk. Tall, graceful, wearing a long leopard fur coat and stilettos.

My claws snag the carpet.

Women's hands in the audience clutch their partner's arms. Another model sashays onto the stage, this time wearing a leopard-fur crop top and miniskirt. My eyes zone in on her belly chain with a leopard tooth hanging from it.

Ethan grips even tighter. I could so easily twist around

and bite his hand. *Am I seriously considering hurting my friend?* I take deep breaths.

Models wrapped in jaguar appear next. My muscles tense. *That could be me! That could be Storm!* They're followed by crocodile, cheetah, snake, snow leopard. *Don't they realize they're modelling mass murder?*

Then the music gets louder and a girl draped in a South China tiger cape walks on. She rubs the collar lovingly. The audience pound their hands and feet.

Without a second thought, I pull out of Ethan's grasp. Soundlessly I run to the stage and leap. Gasps fly from the audience. The model freezes. The clapping stops. I stalk towards her and grab the fur cloak in my jaws. It slips off her back, falling to the floor like it's been shot. The model hurtles offstage. The audience shuffles uncomfortably.

That's when I feel it.

Turning slowly around, I find Delgado pointing a gun at me. *Seriously? He's going to kill me here in front of everyone?* The audience gasp some more and lean forwards. I feel their excitement building. They think it's part of the show!

Lowering my back, I get ready to pounce, when Delgado's eyes widen. But he's not looking at me; he's looking over my head. His face pales and the gun drops to his side. Jerking around, I see a bundle of black and white fur. A skunk. *Where did he come from?* The skunk glares at Delgado, anger flaring in his eyes. Then he glances at me. I know what he's telling me. *Go!*

Bounding off the stage, I head straight for the exit.

Members of the audience start screaming as I run past. *You only like me dead!* I growl. Bursting into fresh air, I realize the furs didn't make me sick. As a jaguar, they had no effect.

I stop in the road. No one's about. *Please say Ethan followed me.* Then I smell him. And soon I see him running towards me.

'I got it all—the show, the audience, Delgado,' he says, waving his mobile in the air. 'I'm uploading it now. YouTube, Twitter, Facebook.'

I nod and leave Ethan standing.

'Hey—where are you going?' he demands.

Does he honestly think I can answer? I'm a cat!

CHAPTER
THIRTY-SEVEN

Racing to the nearest car park, I storm straight into the cramped valet parking hut. Two men yell. I snarl and they run from the building. Any minute now they'll be back with a guard. And a gun. Leaping onto the desk, I grab the nearest key fob in my mouth. I don't care which of the guests it belongs to, but I'm hoping it's a good car. Ethan deserves to drive in a Ferrari for what he's done.

Padding back outside, I look up to see if there's any CCTV. But I can't spot a camera. Great for me. I stare into the side mirror of the closest car, and my ears and fur recede. Opening my mouth, the key fob falls to my hand. Half walking, half jogging down the rows, I aim the key fob at different cars. On the fourth row, lights flicker and I hear a beep.

197

A silver two-seater Aston Martin. Ethan will be pleased.

I put on gloves. Checking no one's around, I open the door and drop into the black leather seat. The car purrs to life and I head back to where I left Ethan. He's standing next to a tree looking around, looking lost. I pull up next to him and his jaw drops. Less than a second later, he's in the car, stroking the dashboard.

'Don't touch. You're not wearing gloves,' I say.

'Can I borrow yours?'

'If you plan to drive.'

His eyes sparkle. 'I didn't know that was an option.'

'It's not!'

We see a few employees but no guests as we drive to the hotel's exit. The barrier's down and there's a guard sitting in the booth next to it.

'How are we going to get past him?' asks Ethan.

I slam my foot down on the accelerator.

'What are you doing? We'll crash!' yells Ethan.

We hurtle towards the bar stretching across the road.

'Hold on,' I shout, bracing myself, when the barrier lifts automatically.

Swooping under it, we race down the causeway.

'Wahoo!' shrieks Ethan. Then he turns his head. 'The guard's watching.'

'He probably thinks we're a pair of rich ponces showing off in our car.'

'I thought you didn't want to attract attention.'

'Being too young to drive would attract attention too.'

It takes a few attempts to find the motel—we get lost twice—but finally we unlock the door to our room. We stare around in horror. It's been cleaned. And the suitcase is missing.

'My laptop,' yelps Ethan.

'I'm going to reception.'

A fat middle-aged man, resembling a toad, sits behind the desk. 'Yeah, we have your bag. You didn't hand in your key,' he says, his jowls wobbling.

'I'm really sorry—we were in a rush. Here it is,' I say, putting the key onto the table.

'You gotta pay for another night.'

'But we're not staying another night.'

He shrugs. 'You're checking out late. If you want your bag, you gotta pay.' His already narrow eyes squeeze even smaller as he looks between the pair of us. 'How old are you guys anyway?'

I slam the money on the table and the man smirks. He disappears into a back room before returning with my suitcase.

'No one's been in it, have they?' asks Ethan.

'Why? What you got in there?' says the man, eyeing us even more suspiciously.

Without answering, we rush back to the Aston Martin. Lugging the suitcase into the boot, Ethan unzips it and sighs with relief. He pulls out his laptop, sits in the passenger seat and starts tapping away. Still wearing gloves, I transfer the Dagger of Eztli and my tools into the suitcase. I hate letting go of such precious items, but they won't get past security in hand luggage.

'How are you getting on?' I ask, joining Ethan in the front of the car.

'You are not going to believe this,' he says breathlessly. 'There's a plane to Heathrow in just over an hour.'

'You're kidding me? We're actually having a bit of luck?'

'Yeah. We might even make it to school on time.'

School? I hadn't even thought about that. 'Can you get us on it?'

'I'm trying.' Then Ethan turns to me, his eyes twinkling. 'Have a look at my phone. The videos have gone viral. Thousands of hits. Loads of audience members from the show have been named. People are calling for the police to take action, especially against the Delgados.'

'That's brilliant.' Then my insides spiral. 'Do you think Delgado will tell the police about my dad?'

Ethan shakes his head. 'Delgado isn't going to want to get in any more trouble. He's not going to admit to employing a cat burglar. Anyway, the dagger has nothing to do with the fashion show.'

'I hope you're right,' I mutter. More loudly I say, 'Can I see the footage?'

While he continues working on getting plane tickets, I watch the fashion show. I see the jaguar leap on stage—*I really am majestic as a wildcat*—and see Delgado get the gun. But as I watch, I realize something's missing.

'Ethan, did you see a skunk on stage?'

'A what?' He looks up, frowning.

'A sku—' I stop. 'Don't worry about it.' For now I know what Delgado's real Nahualli is. And it wasn't happy.

'Booked the tickets!' says Ethan triumphantly.

Five hours later Ethan and I are on the plane in first class, heading home. Buying top-price tickets let us check in late, and now we're huddled over his laptop, reading the news. '*Storm and Thunder reunited*' is the headline. There's a movie clip where two jaguars see each other again for the first time. I have to wipe my eyes at least twice. Ethan's pretending he has a cold.

'We did do the right thing, didn't we?' he says suddenly. 'Getting him back to the zoo, instead of setting him free?'

'I've been thinking about that too, but I don't think Storm would survive in the wild. He'd need too much rehabilitation. And look at the pair of them, rolling around together. They're so happy.'

A revolving banner suddenly appears at the bottom of the screen. Breaking news: Melinda and Anton Delgado arrested for poaching and skinning endangered animals.

'Ethan, you are a genius,' I say.

'*We* are geniuses,' he corrects.

He grabs my hand and squeezes. I don't pull away.

CHAPTER THIRTY-EIGHT

I sink deeper into the huge, comfortable plane seat, my eyelids growing heavy. I want to stay awake, talk about the fashion show, the ceremony, but exhaustion takes over. My eyes close and I drift into blackness . . .

Suddenly I'm in a stone temple, standing before an altar. A fire burns and flickers in front of me, heating the cauldron on top. Four masked priests stand on the opposite side. I am Achcauhtli—their leader, the highest of all high priests. With a long staff, I stir a mixture of bubbling gold and blood. Our blood. Inhaling the vapour, my nerves tingle. Not lo̶n̶g̶ ̶n̶ow and the bracelet will be forged. The powers ̶o̶f̶ ̶t̶h̶e̶ ̶N̶ahuallis will run through my veins. I will b̶e̶ ̶a̶b̶l̶e̶ ̶t̶o̶ ̶s̶hift into an eagle, a jaguar, a— ̶ ̶ ̶ ̶ ̶ ̶ ̶ ̶ ̶ ̶ ̶plunging the room into darkness.

̶ ̶ ̶ ̶ ̶ ̶ ̶ ̶ ̶ ̶my law!' shrieks a voice. The words

bounce off the walls of the temple. I cover my ears and fall to my knees.

'You dare disobey me, the god of the sun.'

A blinding light appears. I squint to witness a serpent emerge through the white. I bow my head so low it touches the cold floor.

'The new day is about to start,' he roars. 'The beginning of the new cycle.'

I lift my head in horror. 'It can't be,' I whisper.

Has the forging of the bracelet taken that long? We had a whole day before the New Fire Ceremony begins.

'All flames should be extinguished,' shrieks the serpent. 'And you, Achcauhtli, as the highest of all high priests, should be on the hill, lighting the first fire. Yet you are here.'

I open my mouth, finding no words.

'From this day forth, you are banished from the hillside.'

I look back at the ground, but summon all my courage. 'Our noble god, we have done you great wrong. But you must realize why. We are forging the bracelet to stop the Spanish. They are killing us.'

'Will the bracelet be any good to you if the sun does not rise? You will be dead anyway.'

Silence echoes around the chamber.

Finally the serpent speaks: 'I will allow the bracelet to be finished and you, the five priests, may live. But understand this: never will the bracelet work where there is smoke.'

The light disappears. We are plummeted back into darkness.

I feel a jolt—like my head's being shaken. Has the sun god returned? Am I being punished some more? My head shakes again and my eyes flash open. My head is on Ethan's shoulder and he's lifting it up and down.

'We're here,' he says. 'You drooled on my top!'

Going through security, waiting for our luggage, finding a taxi all pass in a blur. Part of me can't stop thinking about my dream; the other part just wants to collapse. I don't think I've ever felt this exhausted. Ethan and I utter about five words during the entire taxi ride back to Somerset.

The driver drops Ethan off at school and then me at home. As expected, Dad's car isn't on the driveway.

I call, 'Dad,' just in case, as I slip in through the front door.

There's no reply.

I drag my suitcase to my room. My bed looks so inviting but I've only got about twenty minutes before school starts. I slide the tools under my bed, before using a T-shirt to pick up the Dagger of Etzli. Even through the material, it makes my skin crawl.

I don't want this thing in my house, especially in my room. But what can I do with it? There's no way Delgado's getting it back. I can't give it to a museum—he might steal it again. Should I destroy it?

Can I destroy a priceless relic?

The clock's ticking, so I shove the dagger into my underwear drawer—Dad will never look there—and jump in the shower. With wet hair, I leap on my bike and pedal as fast as I can to school. I head up the steps just as the bell goes. I'm not the only one late. There are loads of teenagers rushing inside. It seems very strange when your world has turned upside down—you've been chased, shot at, left to burn in a fire—and yet you return to school as if nothing has happened. The world's kept turning for everyone else and they have absolutely no idea what you've been going through.

I pass a group of sniggering girls from the year below and drop my head like usual. My hair falls over my face when suddenly I think of the airport and Ethan's words: 'They're going to stare at you anyway.'

I stop and turn to look at them.

One of the girls pulls out a mirror and starts pouting. As if I do that??? The others burst out laughing. A few days ago I would have shuffled off, not wanting to attract extra attention. But clearly that method is not working. And so I channel my inner jaguar. I don't need my wrist to strangle or my body to heat. Glaring at the girl with the mirror, I lift my lips into a snarl. The group falls silent. Their eyes widen. Their faces pale. Good!

Holding my head high, I walk down the corridor. So this is how I'll survive school. From now on, I'm going to have to look at everyone as if I'm planning to eat them.

I walk into form room. Zac is sitting in my usual seat with Olivia draped over the desk in front of him, laughing inanely at something he said.

I march straight up to him. 'I'd like my seat back, please.'

He leans back his head and smiles smugly. 'Does it have your name on it?'

I pull out a pencil and scribble Scarlet on to the back of the chair. 'Yes, it does.'

Gasps fly around the room.

'I bet she wants to add your name too, with a love heart,' says Olivia.

'Or maybe she wants to kick you both out of her seat and would be happy if neither of you ever speak to her again.' I say.

I boot the table harder than I planned. It judders and for a horrible moment I think I've broken it, but thankfully it remains in one piece. Olivia leaps up.

'In fact why do you want to sit here? Does it remind you of me?' I say.

Zac jumps up too. 'If you want it that much, have it. Didn't realize we were in primary school.'

I lean forward, my eyes flashing and I can feel my lips pulling back. Zac steps away.

'Leave me alone. And leave frogs alone,' I snarl.

Blinking rapidly, he straightens his back. 'Freak,' he says.

Other kids mutter 'freak' too but they don't look at me. And I couldn't care less what they think, what they say about me, as long as they leave me alone. I flop into my seat and rummage in my bag. I must have a rubber in here somewhere. I'll have to get rid of the pencil mark when everyone's gone. I hate destroying property.

CHAPTER THIRTY-NINE

By the end of the school day, I'm even more exhausted. I can't quite believe what's happened in the last seventy-two hours. I pedal slowly home, then spot Dad's car on the drive. He's early. I thought he was coming home this evening.

'You're back,' I say, bursting through the front door.

'I've only been away a weekend,' he says, stepping out from the kitchen into the hallway.

'How was the heist?'

'Great,' he says. My insides shrink. It must have shown on my face because he adds, 'I missed you, though. Could have done with you as lookout.'

'Did you get the Chinese sculpture? Can I see it?'

'I've already sent it,' he says.

'Already?'

'Like I told you, it was a rush job.' He hesitates. 'So how was your weekend at Ethan's gran's?'

I take a deep breath. 'I didn't go.'

'I beg your pardon?'

'I didn't go. I didn't want to.'

'What do you mean you didn't want to?' he explodes.

'I decided to stay here.'

'You stayed here on your own?' Then his face darkens even more. 'Or was Ethan here too?'

'No!'

'So if I call his school, they'll say he was there all weekend?'

'OK, he was here too.'

Dad jabs his finger at me and I don't think I've ever seen him this angry. 'You stayed the whole weekend on your own with your boyfriend?'

'He is not my boyfriend!'

'Have you—' his face contorts in horror '—kissed?'

'Ugh! No.'

For a split second, Dad's lips twitch and he looks relieved. Then he remembers how angry he is with me.

'Dad, I couldn't face watching all those TV programmes. You know that's all his gran does. I would have had to spend the whole weekend watching soap operas. You always say too much TV is bad for you.'

His eyebrow rise.

'And I just wanted to be here,' I say.

'You packed your suitcase.'

'I unpacked it as soon as you'd gone. We got Ethan's

gran out of the house so you wouldn't take me over. Then Ethan's sister rang her to say that we went to hers.'

'Ethan's sister is involved—why am I not surprised?' He folds his arms. 'You're the little master criminals, aren't you?'

'You should be pleased I'm telling you the truth. I could have lied and pretended I'd gone to his gran's.'

'Except I was going to take Mrs Riley some flowers, so that wouldn't have worked.'

And that's why I'm telling you now.

'But I am pleased you're telling me the truth.' He rubs his forehead. 'You are, however, grounded forever.'

'I expected that,' I say. Actually I never want to leave my room again, especially my bed.

'Grounded means Ethan can't come here either,' says Dad.

'What?'

'I'm not sure he's the greatest influence on you.'

'But Ethan's my best friend. I need him.'

Dad doesn't look convinced.

'And I can see you how you might need someone else too,' I add. 'Like Juliet.'

His eyes widen.

'So I was thinking—if you want to invite her over for another meal, I promise to be on my best behaviour.'

'Does best behaviour mean you won't interrogate or attack her?'

'As long as she doesn't wear fur.'

'I'm sure she'll never wear fur again.'

'Then I like her more already.'

Dad smiles and looks skyward for a second. 'You're really growing up. I wish your mum could see it.'

I wish she could too.

'And just so you know, I missed you on this last heist,' he says. 'Next time you can come with me.'

'Do you have another one set up?'

'No. But when I do, I'm going to let you be lookout again. You've got one last chance to prove yourself. But there can be no more rule-breaking. Can I trust you?'

'Of course,' I say looking him straight in the eyes.

It's getting easier and easier to lie to Dad. I'm not sure that's a good thing.

CHAPTER FORTY

Three hours later, I'm in the woods behind our house. Dad had to go out and I promised to stay in. Technically I'm not disobeying him. These are our grounds . . . sort of.

I stare at the Dagger of Eztli lying on the earthy floor in front of me. All I have to do is drop the rock. But my hands seem frozen in the air, my fingers refusing to open.

Come on—this dagger is evil!

It's no use. I can't destroy it.

Stepping back, I lower the rock to the ground. What the hell am I going to do with it? Then I twist around and run to the house. Grabbing a spade, I return to the woods and find a spot hidden amongst the trees. I start to dig. The ground's not too hard. Apparently it rained all weekend.

'You're not burying someone, are you?'

I jump, spinning round at the same time. The spade high in the air, ready to slam down on someone's head.

Ethan leaps backwards. 'Don't kill me either!'

'Don't frighten me like that, then,' I say, lowering the spade. 'What are you doing here anyway? Shouldn't you be at school?'

Ethan bites back a smile. 'I've been suspended.'

'What?'

'They found out I snuck out and so I've been suspended for a week. Mum's in America, Dad can't take the time off, so I've been shipped to Gran's.'

My stomach twists. 'I am so sorry.'

He shrugs. 'It was worth it.'

'Are your parents mad?'

'On a scale of one to hundred, I'd say we're topping a thousand.'

Oh God!

'What are you digging for?' he asks, looking at the hole. 'Treasure?'

I nudge the dagger with my shoe. 'I can't destroy a priceless artefact.'

'So you're hiding it?'

I nod.

'Good idea,' says Ethan. 'And I've got some fab news. Dad told me the police have stopped searching for it.'

'Why?'

'No new clues. The case is dead.'

'That's great.'

'You want me to help you dig?'

Ethan finds a second spade in my house, and half an hour later, the Dagger of Eztli lies buried deep in the ground.

He tilts his head. 'So . . . do you think an evil dagger tree will grow?'

'Ugh—don't tempt fate. Nothing will surprise me when it comes to Aztec magic.' I throw the spade onto the ground and turn to look at him. 'You know what? I think it's about time you learned how to climb a tree.'

He stares at me. Stunned. 'Now? Aren't you exhausted?'

'Really . . . I'm trying to hide you in case Dad gets back. I'm grounded and you're not allowed here.'

I grab the branches of an oak tree and show him where I put my feet. I climb slowly, letting Ethan copy. He's not too bad. More like a chicken than a giraffe. We sit hidden on a bough.

'Your Dad's mad at me, then?' says Ethan.

'He says you're a bad influence.'

'*Me?*'

'Well, obviously it was all your doing—stopping me going to your gran's.'

'Hah!' he snorts.

I lift my wrist and look at where the bracelet would be.

'Still wish you'd never put it on?' he asks.

'Actually, I'm beginning to trust it. I think the bracelet only lets me transform when I really need to, as long as there isn't smoke. '

'So you don't hate it any more?'

'No, I think I should listen to it a bit more.' I lean against the trunk. 'Life is actually looking up. School isn't bad. Dad and I are getting on. We even had a heart to heart.'

'You told him about Delgado?'

'No. I wish I could.'

'Did he tell you about this weekend?'

'Yeah. He got the Chinese statuette.'

Ethan looks at me out of the corner of his eyes. 'So you're both lying, then?'

'What?'

'Nothing.' His eyes dart left, a sign of lying.

'Tell me.'

'It's nothing.' His foot starts tapping.

'Now I know you're lying. What is it?'

'I don't know whether I should say. You look really happy for once.'

'I'm always really happy,' I snap. 'Spit it out.'

Ethan starts spiking up his hair. 'All right. This morning I found out where your dad was. It was on his laptop.'

'That's great news. It means he doesn't think anyone's bugging his computer.' Ethan looks uneasy and a cold chill spreads through me. 'Where was he?' I ask.

He takes a deep breath. 'He *was* in Spain but there wasn't a heist. He went to a wedding with Juliet. I found an email. He was apologizing for your behaviour at a dinner. Your dad agreed to go to the wedding as a way of saying sorry.'

The world spins. I grab onto the tree.

'I'm sorry,' whispers Ethan. 'But you lied to him too.'

I know that!

'At least you know you can always trust me,' he adds.

'I guess,' I say. Then something comes back to me. 'Except I can't always trust you, can I? Did you think I forgot how you pushed me out of a tree in the Everglades?'

'But I knew you'd transform. I've done so much research.'

'You pushed me into a moat full of alligators.'

'Let's talk more about your dad. How he went away with Juliet. He's the one you're really angry with.'

'I could have died.'

'I thought you were going to be an eagle. It didn't occur to me you'd be a reptile. You were really small, by the way. The runt of the litter.'

'Do you think this is helping your case?'

'But if I hadn't pushed you, you wouldn't have got into Delgado's estate. You wouldn't have found out where they were keeping Storm.'

'I'd have found out another way.'

'You were so distressed. I was thinking of you.'

I snort.

'And I've been looking into alligators. Did you know they're supposed to be really wise? According to the Aztecs, they were there when the world was formed so they have vast knowledge. I've given you knowledge.'

'Yeah? Well, when I was an alligator I didn't feel very wise. I think I was spending too much time trying to survive.' I jab my finger at him. 'And you couldn't know for sure that I would transform. I could be dead right now.'

'That's not true. You said it yourself: if there's no smoke around, you always transform if you need to.'

Suddenly Ethan leans forward and shoves me. I drop straight out of the tree.

'You're going to fly!' he yells . . .

As I land with a thud.

My legs crumple beneath me and I scream out in agony.

'Scar,' he cries, scrabbling down the tree.

Pain throbs through my legs. My wrist tightens and the skin on my hands bubbles. I think of Ethan and what I want to do to him.

'Ethan, run!' I shout. But the words come out in a roar.

Maybe I shouldn't trust the bracelet after all.

ABOUT THE AUTHOR

Tamsin loves to travel, have adventures, and see wild animals. She's fed a tiger, held a seven-foot python and stroked a tarantula, but she's too scared to touch a worm. She lives in Somerset with her adrenalin-junkie family. When she isn't writing, she can be found reading books, eating jellybeans, or tromping through the woods with her soppy dog.

Top ten interesting facts according to Ethan

The Golden Eagle

• Force of talons compares to the force of a bullet. (Don't make Scar mad when she's an eagle!)

• Wingspan is about the length of a polar bear.

• They can see so many more shades of colour than humans can, helping them spot camouflaged prey. Have been known to see a rabbit two miles away!

• Eagles prefer to eat fresh meat rather than animals that are already dead. They eat birds and small mammals. They've been known to kill foxes, goats, and deer.

• Can fly at 30 mph. When diving for prey, they can get to speeds of 150 mph.

• Threats are: shooting, poisoning, egg-collecting, nest destruction, and collision with power lines. (And airport security!)

Jaguars

- Jaguars are the third largest cats in the world. From the top of their nose to the tip of its tail, a jaguar can be the size of a car.
- Their fur is usually tan or orange with black spots called rosettes because they look like roses.
- The name 'jaguar' comes from the Native American word 'yaguar' which means 'he who kills with one leap'. (This doesn't surprise me!)
- They eat a rich diet of meat and fish, such as deer, crocodiles, snakes, monkey, deer, sloths, tapir, turtles, eggs, frogs, fish, and anything else they can catch. Hopefully not humans!
- Can run up to 64mph over short distances. Almost motorway speed!
- The jaguar hunts mainly on the ground, but it can climb a tree and pounce on its prey from above. Usually it kills its prey with one crushing bite to the skull.
- Jaguars love water—they swim, play, and even hunt for fish in streams and ponds. They wave their tails over the surface to attract the fish.
- Jaguars are nocturnal, lounging about in the day, then hunting at night. (Pretty much like Scar—lounging at school, cat burglar at night!)

The American Alligator

- Alligators are dark, almost black. Their skin is thick, covered in bony plates like armour. Unlike a crocodile, their fourth tooth is hidden. (Not sure I'll get that close to Scar to check!)

- They are opportunistic feeders, eating pretty much anything. Fish, birds, turtles, snakes . . . They eat animals whole, and can drag a larger creature into the water to make them drown!

- The largest male recorded in Florida grew to 14 ft. ^{1}/2 inch. Female alligators rarely grow larger than 10 ft. (That's all right, then!)

- Alligators are bred on farms for their meat and skin. It's a huge multi million-dollar business. (Somehow I don't think Scar would let me try the meat!)

- They were endangered, but are now thriving because of changes in the law. Over a million in the wild now!

- Alligators have lived on the planet for millions of years and are sometimes called 'Living fossils'. (Scar—you're a living fossil!!)

ACKNOWLEDGEMENTS

Ooh—there are so many people who have really helped me write this book and I want to say a huge thank you to them all.

Anne Clark, my fabulous agent, for giving me endless support and encouragement.

My editors Clare Whitston and Gill Sore, who really deserve their own superhero capes. They helped me make *Mission Gone Wild* the best it can be. Lizzie Smart for creating the brilliant book covers—I love their shininess. In fact, I'd like to thank everyone at OUP. I feel incredibly lucky to be part of such a marvellous team.

My amazing husband, Graham, for giving me the time to write, putting up with my strange sleep patterns and taking me to the Everglades.

My wonderful kids, Toby and Daisy, for continuing to inspire me and making me laugh.

My mum, Violetta. Even though she's no longer here, she always supported me and gave me self-belief.

My Dad, for reading stories to me when I was little and correcting my grammar (he still does!).

My sister, Pia, who shares my love of stories and is passionate about the strength of words.

To Jen and Pete, my in-laws, for their enthusiasm and encouragement.

My friends Pip Sear and Helen Jones for letting me bounce ideas off them on our long dog walks or over coffee and cake. My friends Ruth, Floss, Eileen, Charlotte, Nic, and Sophie. I feel like I have my own cheerleading squad. I'm so grateful to have such fabulous friends.

And finally, there are many more family members and friends I'd like to thank. I can't begin to name them all and, besides, they know who they are . . .

Jo Clarke, an amazing book blogger, for her incredible support and promotion of The Scarlet Files.

THE SHAPESHIFTING BEGINS IN . . .

THE SCARLET FILES

CAT BURGLAR

Schoolgirl by day, cat burglar by night . . .

TAMSIN COOKE

TURN THE PAGE TO READ
THE FIRST CHAPTER . . .

CHAPTER ONE

I lie flat against the edge of the roof, my senses on high alert. Come on, Dad, where are you? Surely it shouldn't take this long to see if a room is clear. Then a hand clutches my shoulder and my body jumps. Somehow I manage not to fall off the three-storey house. I stare at Dad in amazement. How can he be so quiet? I haven't heard a footstep or even a scuffle on the tiles.

Dad swoops over the lip of the roof, dropping to the second floor balcony below. This is it—the moment I've been waiting for. I take a deep breath and scramble over the guttering. With fingers clinging to the roof, I dangle nine and a half metres above the ground. Adrenalin surging, I swing my legs and hurtle though the air before landing, knees bent, beside him. I rub my arms and stretch out my fingers.

Dad and I are dressed the same—black overalls, balaclavas, thin leather gloves, and rucksacks. Our night-vision goggles make the world green. Together we stare through the glass double doors. The room in front of us is empty, but the owners are sleeping in the next bedroom. Have we woken them? I hate to admit it, but my landing was much louder than Dad's.

Thankfully no lights appear, and Dad picks the lock in the door. Reaching into my back pocket, I pull out a sliver of foil. I hand it to Dad and watch him use it to block the sensor. He slides the door open a fraction, and when the alarm doesn't go off, he yanks it further on its rails.

Dad creeps into the house first and I follow closely behind. He shuts the balcony door, while I take stock of the room. Everything is exactly where I expect it to be—the double bed, the rug, the chest of drawers, the mask, and the jewellery box. Dad's plans were perfect.

I step forward when Dad grabs hold of my arm and jabs his index finger at the large oval rug. My mouth dries. I can't believe I forgot. I give him a quick thumbs-up.

We grab the edge of the rug and carefully roll it back, to reveal small pressure pads dotted about on the carpet. If I'd stepped on one of those, an alarm would have exploded somewhere. Most of the pads are clustered below the spot where the Aztec mask is hanging. Even through my night-vision goggles, the mask looks horrible, frightening. I'm not sure how anyone could sleep with that thing staring down at them.

2

I watch Dad navigate the room. He pulls some tweezers out of his bag and starts fiddling with various wires. While he deactivates an alarm attached to the mask, I tiptoe across the carpet, avoiding the few pressure pads in my path. My target, the jewellery box, is on top of the chest of drawers. According to Dad's plans, the box is free from alarms, but I finger the area just in case. Good—there are no wires or signs of extra security.

Tilting the wooden lid, I find the box stuffed with brooches, bracelets, and necklaces. I ease some of it to one side when I hear a noise. I freeze. There's another noise—a creak. Someone, somewhere in the house, is moving. I hardly dare breathe. My eyes dart between the door to the landing and Dad, who stands motionless with the Aztec mask in one hand. Dad lifts his free hand, holding it out in front of him. I know what he's telling me: Don't panic. Don't move.

I stay still. Feet scuff the carpet on the landing. Now should we bolt? Again I glance at Dad, but his hand remains in the air. The footsteps pass our door, but that doesn't mean we're safe. What if it's someone collecting a cricket bat to bash us over the heads with? Or phoning the police? I hear a click, and a soft glow of light appears from under the door to the landing. Then I catch the sound of tinkling. I let out a quiet sigh. It's just someone going to the toilet.

Still I don't move and neither does Dad. The tinkling seems to be endless. Finally, I hear a chain flush and a click, and the glow disappears. The footsteps begin again, passing our room, and a bed creaks as someone climbs into it. Dad's hand is still flat against the air. My muscles ache from being so tense. I know he's waiting for the person to fall back to sleep. But really? Do we have to wait this long? At last Dad changes his flat hand into a thumbs-up and twists back around.

As quietly as I can, I dive back into the jewellery box, this time rummaging with more speed. Soon my eyes fall upon a thick bracelet covered in precious stones and I can't contain my grin. I've found it! Fingers shaking, I lift the bracelet, wrap it up in a square of black velvet, and slip it into the front pocket of my rucksack. I pull out an exact replica and stuff it in the bottom of the box. Then I carefully pile on the rest of the jewellery, trying to remember the order in which I took it out. A beaded necklace and dragonfly brooch were definitely on the top. I close the lid, and wipe down every surface I touched. Stepping back, I examine my work. No one will notice . . . hopefully.

I turn around to see Dad reactivating the alarm, now attached to a fake mask hanging on the wall. He wipes down the whole area before hopping over the pressure pads. I meet him by the double bed and together we unroll the rug. Dad studies the room and nods. He uses the foil to stop the sensor, and signals for me to open the door. Slipping outside, I wait for him to join me out on the balcony.

I feel lightheaded. The tension drains away. I can't believe I stole the bracelet . . . all on my own!

4

Dad relocks the glass doors, as I hoist the rucksack onto my shoulders. Together, under the moonlit sky, we climb over the railings and swing onto the first floor balcony. Without pausing, we leap over another set of railings and drop to the ground. No streetlights—we run to our black car and jump inside.

Dad drives two streets away, before saying, 'NVGs.'

I tear off my night-vision goggles and Dad does the same. He puts on the headlights.

'So what do you think? How did I do?' I burst.

'You were great,' says Dad.

I clasp my gloved hands together. 'When can I do it again?'

'Soon,' says Dad. 'But right now, I think you should try to get some sleep. After all, you do have school tomorrow.'

PRAISE FOR 'THE SCARLET FILES: CAT BURGLAR'

'Full of twists and turns. I think the characters
were extremely interesting.'
Saskia, 11

'Suspense, thrills, imagination, and surprises
leaping from page to page . . . I want to be able
to shapeshift myself!'
Imi, 11

'Scar is so adventurous and amazing.
I loved her character.'
Kate, 11

'Great characters. Scar is different to
any other girl I've ever met.'
Amy, 10

'Scar's adventures are so daring,
dangerous, and full of surprises!!'
Rebecca, 10

'Full of adventure . . . lures you into a world of
mystery where literally anything can happen.'
Eve, 12

'A really exhilarating read.'
Connie, 11

'It's excellent! . . . the characters really come to
life and you feel as if you really know them'.
Matilda, 12

CR 6/16

Ready for more great stories?
Try one of these ...

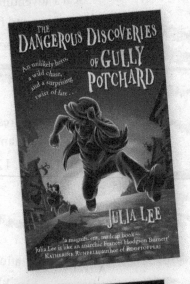

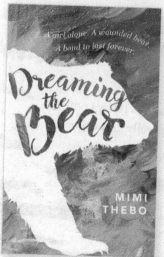